Fanny Hill
or, Memoirs of a Woman of Pleasure
VOLUME II

THE SCARLET LIBRARY
LONDON MMIV

THE SCARLET LIBRARY

is an imprint of
THE *Erotic* Print Society
EPS, 17 Harwood Road,
LONDON SW6 4QP

Tel (UK only): 0871 7110 134
Outside UK: +44 (0)20 7736 5800
Fax: +44 (0)1235 824358
Email: *eros@eroticprints.org*.
Web: *www.eroticprints.org*

ISBN: 1-898998-91-4
Printed and bound in Spain by Bookprint, S.L., Barcelona
© 2004 MacHo Ltd, London UK

No part of this publication may be reproduced by
any means without the express written permission of
the Publishers. The moral right of the author of the
designated drawings has been asserted.

Fanny Hill
or, Memoirs of a Woman of Pleasure
VOLUME II

John Cleland

with new illustrations by
Erich von Götha

The Scarlet Library

CONTENTS

7 FOREWORD
9 ABOUT THE ARTIST

SECOND LETTER

11 PART VI
42 PART VII
68 PART VIII
94 PART IX
120 PART X

FOREWORD

THE BOOK
John Cleland (1709-89), born of a family of ancient Scottish lineage, was educated at Westminster School in London. His early life was, from a career point of view, promising. As a young man he became consul in Smyrna, then travelled to Bombay to work in the East India Company; leaving India, he spent much time in wandering and travel on the Continent, but about the time he returned to London, his father died and it seems that he first became acquainted with financial hardship. He eked out a precarious existence as a freelance literary journalist occasionally slipping into serious debt. Indeed, when he put the finishing touches to *Memoirs of a Woman of Pleasure* (now more popularly known as *Fanny Hill*), it was purported to be from the inside of a debtor's gaol.

Published in two parts in 1748-9, the book enjoyed an enormous success. It is said that although it earned Cleland's publisher £10,000 (a vast sum in those days), the author received a mere 20 guineas. In reality his publisher, Ralph Griffiths, only sold 750 copies of the first edition (if you find one, let me know) and he and Cleland went on to publish a more commercially successful, but much sanitised version in 1750 entitled *The Memoirs of Fanny Hill*. The year before he had been summoned before the Privy Council for indecency; nothing came of this and a subsequent arrest, indeed, the outcome of his literary prosecutions seem to have done Cleland no harm at all. It was the sort of publicity for his book that a literary agent can only dream of and for some reason best known to themselves, the Government of the day decided to award him an annuity of a £100 for the rest of his relatively long life.

Cleland's early literary success was short-lived. He never again wrote a best seller. In 1751 he published *The Memoirs of a Coxcomb*, and in 1764 *The Surprises of Love*. He wrote various plays, engaged in much journalistic work, and between 1766 and 1769, published three philological studies, with special reference to Celtic.

Unlike Daniel Defoe's famous literary whore, Moll Flanders, Frances Hill is only narrowly developed as a character. Moreover, Fanny is not held up as a pious example of moral decline as is Moll or the 'Harlot' in Hogarth's famous series of etchings. Cleland's heroine is clearly a product of the Enlightenment, but she is found at the more liberal end of its spectrum. He uses her letters and journals skilfully, not only to give highly detailed (and somewhat pornographic) physical descriptions of the more intimate parts of the human body and their actions, but also to report upon the erotic obsessions and peccadilloes of London society. He balances this with the occasional (and wonderfully disingenuous) moral outburst; his use of elaborate euphemisms for describing the basics of sex results in a style that seems to be very much tongue-in-cheek, yet pleasingly erotic, despite the author's protestations to the contrary. The gentle parody may have amused some of his contemporary readers, but the majority would have found Fanny's more racy passages deeply shocking (and no doubt highly arousing). This fine balance of near-satire and sexually implicit prose has kept the novel alive down the centuries and those readers who are prepared to make the effort of overcoming the unfamiliarity of mid-18th century language will be amply rewarded.

THE ARTIST

The background and identity of the elusive Erich von Götha

is the stuff of legend. It has been claimed by various ill-informed sources that he is a German diplomat, a Russian Doctor, a well-known French philosopher, or an English academic named Robbins. There are elements of truth in all these stories, but not much. He was always destined to become an artist; he completed his education with four years training in London.

Quickly discovering a predilection for the erotic and sometimes obscene depiction of beautiful women, often particularly appreciated by women themselves, he contributed to early editions of *The Sex Maniac's Diary*. From then he went on to produce his own ground-breaking magazine, *Torrid*, long since disappeared but now avidly collected. Disgusted by his treatment at the hands of the publishers (when he left them, they told callers he had died) and frustrated by censorship in England, he needed the fateful words of an Irish psychic and the strange and still baffling intervention of an Italian benefactor – Mozart's 'Man In Black' obviously comes to mind – before finding his publishing home in France. After publication of *The Troubles of Janice* he swiftly gained a world-wide reputation (the book is still available today everywhere except the UK). In the past two years he has had exhibitions of his work in Paris, Brussels and Bologna and is recognised by some of the more outré of critics as one of the seminal figures in the evolution of BDA (bande dessinée adulte), a barely perceptible branch in the history of Conceptual Art. One reviewer wrote about the *Janice* tetralogy that it was an allegory of the Manichean world view, and that if you buy one book of philosophy this year, make it this one. Not, von Götha decided, serious, nor sarcastic; but very funny and, of course, totally accurate.

Photographs of von Götha do not exist but portraits depict him alternatively with a monocle, bald pate and cruel mouth or with white hair, a genial smile and a twinkle in the eye.

SECOND LETTER
PART VI

Madam,

If I have delay'd the sequel of my history, it has been purely to allow myself a little breathing time not without some hopes that, instead of pressing me to a continuation, you would have acquitted me of the task of pursuing a confession, in the course of which my self-esteem has so many wounds to sustain.

I imagined, indeed, that you would have been cloy'd and tired with uniformity of adventures and expressions, inseparable from a subject of this sort, whose bottom, or groundwork being, in the nature of things, eternally one and the same, whatever variety of forms and modes the situations are susceptible of, there is no escaping a repetition of near the same images, the same figures, the same expressions, with this further inconvenience added to the disgust it creates, that the words *joys, ardours, transports, ecstasies,* and the rest of those pathetic terms so congenial to, so received in the *practise of pleasure,* flatten and lose much of their due spirit and energy by the frequency they indispensably recur with, in a narrative of which that *practice* professedly composes the whole basis. I must therefore trust to the candour of your judgement, for your allowing for the disadvantage I am necessarily under in that respect, and to your imagination and sensibility, the pleasing task of repairing it by their supplements, where my descriptions flag or fail: the one will readily place the pictures I present before your eyes; the other give life to the colours where they are dull, or worn with too frequent handling.

What you say besides, by way of encouragement, concerning the extreme difficulty of continuing so long in one strain, in a mean temper'd with taste, between the revoltingness of gross, rank and vulgar expressions, and the ridicule of mincing metaphors and affected circumlocutions, is so sensible, as well as good-natur'd, that you greatly justify me to myself for my compliance with a curiosity that is to be satisfied so extremely at my expense.

Resuming now where I broke off in my last, I am in my way to remark to you that it was late in the evening before I arriv'd at my new lodgings, and Mrs. Cole, after helping me to range and secure my things, spent the whole evening with me in my apartment, where we supped together, in giving me the best advice and instruction with regard to this new stage of my profession I was now to enter upon; and passing thus from a private devotee to pleasure into a public one, to become a more general good, with all the advantages requisite to put my person out to use, either for interest or pleasure, or both. But then, she observ'd, as I was a kind of new face upon the town, that it was an established rule, and part of trade, for me to pass for a maid, and dispose of myself as such on the first good occasion, without prejudice, however, to such diversions as I might have a mind to in the interim; for that nobody could be a greater enemy than she was to the losing of time. That she would, in the mean time, do her best to find out a proper person, and would undertake to manage this nice point for me, if I would accept of her aid and advice to such good purpose that, in the loss of a fictitious maidenhead, I should reap all the advantages of a native one.

Though such a delicacy of sentiments did not extremely

FANNY HILL VOL II

belong to my character at that time, I confess, against myself, that I perhaps too readily closed with a proposal which my candor and ingenuity gave me some repugnance to: but not enough to contradict the intention of one to whom I had now thoroughly abandoned the direction of all my steps. For Mrs. Cole had, I do not know how unless by one of those unaccountable invincible sympathies that, nevertheless, form the strongest links, especially of female friendship, won and got entire possession of me. On her side, she pretended that a strict resemblance she fancied she saw in me to an only daughter whom she had lost at my age, was the first motive of her taking to me so affectionately as she did. It might be so: there exist as slender motives of attachment that, gathering force from habit and liking, have proved often more solid and durable than those founded on much stronger reasons; but this I know, that tho' I had no other acquaintance with her than seeing her at my lodgings when I lived with Mr. H——, where she had made errands to sell me some millinery ware, she had by degrees insinuated herself so far into my confidence that I threw myself blindly into her hands, and came, at length, to regard, love, and obey her implicitly; and, to do her justice, I never experienc'd at her hands other than a sincerity of tenderness, and care for my interest, hardly heard of in those of her profession. We parted that night, after having settled a perfect unreserv'd agreement; and the next morning Mrs. Cole came, and took me with her to her house for the first time.

Here, at the first sight of things, I found everything breath'd an air of decency, modesty and order.

In the outer parlour, or rather shop, sat three young women, very demurely employ'd on millinery work, which was the cover of a traffic in more precious commodities; but three beautifuller creatures could hardly be seen. Two of them were extremely fair, the eldest not above nineteen; and the third, much about that age, was a piquant brunette, whose black

THE SCARLET LIBRARY

sparkling eyes, and perfect harmony of features and shape, left her nothing to envy in her fairer companions. Their dress too had the more design in it, the less it appeared to have, being in a taste of uniform correct neatness, and elegant simplicity. These were the girls that compos'd the small domestick flock, which my governess train'd up with surprising order and management, considering the giddy wildness of young girls once got upon the loose. But then she never continued any in her house, whom, after a due novitiate, she found untractable, or unwilling to comply with the rules of it. Thus had she insensibly formed a little family of love, in which the members found so sensibly their account, in a rare alliance of pleasure with interest, and of a necessary outward decency with unbounded secret liberty, that Mrs. Cole, who had pick'd them as much for their temper as their beauty, govern'd them with ease to herself and them too.

To these pupils then of hers, whom she had prepar'd, she presented me as a new boarder, and one that was to be immediately admitted to all the intimacies of the house; upon which these charming girls gave me all the marks of a welcome reception, and indeed of being perfectly pleased with my figure, that I could possibly expect from any of my own sex: but they had been effectually brought to sacrifice all jealousy, or competition of charms, to a common interest, and consider'd me a partner that was bringing no despicable stock of goods into the trade of the house. They gathered round me, view'd me on all sides; and as my admission into this joyous troop made a little holiday, the shew of work was laid aside; and Mrs. Cole giving me up, with special recommendation, to their caresses and entertainment, went about her ordinary business of the house.

The sameness of our sex, age, profession, and views soon created as unreserv'd a freedom and intimacy as if we had been for years acquainted. They took and shew'd me the house, their respective apartments, which were furnished with every article of conveniency and luxury; and above all, a spacious drawing-room, where a select revelling band usually met, in general parties of pleasure; the girls supping with their sparks, and acting their wanton pranks with unbounded licentiousness; whilst a defiance of awe, modesty or jealousy were their standing rules, by which, according to the principles of their society, whatever pleasure was lost on the side of sentiment was abundantly made up to the senses in the poignancy of variety, and the charms of ease and luxury. The authors and supporters of this secret institution would, in the height of their humours style themselves the restorers of the golden age and its simplicity of pleasures, before their innocence became so injustly branded with the names of guilt and shame.

As soon then as the evening began, and the shew of a shop was shut, the academy open'd; the mask of mock-modesty was completely taken off, and all the girls deliver'd over to their respective calls of pleasure or interest with their men; and none of that sex was promiscuously admitted, but only such as Mrs. Cole was previously satisfied with their character and discretion. In short, this was the safest, politest, and, at the same time, the most thorough house of accommodation in town: every thing being conducted so that decency made no intrenchment upon the most libertine pleasures, in the practice of which too, the choice familiars of the house had found the secret so rare and difficult, of reconciling even all the refinements of taste and delicacy with the most gross and determinate gratifications of senuality. After having consum'd the morning in the endearments and instructions of my new acquaintance, we went to dinner, when Mrs. Cole, presiding at the head of her club, gave me the first idea of her management and address, in inspiring these girls with so sensible a love and respect for her. There was no stiffness, no reserve, no airs of pique, or little jealousies, but all was unaffectedly gay, cheerful and easy.

After dinner, Mrs. Cole, seconded by the young ladies, acquainted me that there was a chapter to be held that night in form, for the ceremony of my reception into the sisterhood; and in which, with all due reserve to my maidenhead, that was to be occasionally cook'd up for the first proper chapman, I was to undergo a ceremonial of initiation they were sure I should not be displeased with.

Embark'd as I was, and moreover captivated with the charms of my new companions, I was too much prejudic'd in favour of any proposal they could make, to much as hesitate an assent; which, therefore, readily giving in the style of a *carte blanche*, I receiv'd fresh kisses of compliment from them all, in approval of my docility and good nature. Now I was "a sweet girl . . ." I came into things with a "good grace . . ." I was not "affectedly coy . . ." I should be "the pride of the house . . ." and the like.

This point thus adjusted, the young women left Mrs. Cole to talk and concert matters with me: she explained to me that I should be introduc'd, that very evening, to four of her best friends, one of whom she had, according to the custom of the house, favoured with the preference of engaging me in the first party of pleasure; assuring me, at the same time, that they were all young gentlemen agreeable in their persons, and unexceptionable in every respect; that united, and holding together by the band of common pleasures, they composed the chief support of her house, and made very liberal presents to the girls that pleas'd and humour'd them, so that they were, properly speaking, the founders and patrons of this little seraglio. Not but that she had, at proper seasons, other customers to deal with, whom she stood less upon punctilio with than with these; for instance, it was not on one of them she could attempt to pass me for a maid; they were not only too knowing, too much town-bred to bite at such a bait, but they were such generous benefactors to her that it would be unpardonable to think of it.

Amidst all the flutter and emotion which this promise of pleasure, for such I conceiv'd it, stirr'd up in me, I preserved so much of the woman as to feign just reluctance enough to make some merit of sacrificing it to the influence of my patroness, whom I likewise, still in character, reminded of it perhaps being right for me to go home and dress, in favour of my first impressions.

But Mrs. Cole, in opposition to this, assured me that the gentlemen I should be presented to were, by their rank and taste of things, infinitely superior to the being touched with any glare of dress or ornaments, such as silly women rather confound and overlay than set off their beauty with; that these veteran voluptuaries knew better than not to hold them in the highest contempt: they with whom the pure native charms alone could pass current, and who would at any time leave a sallow, washy, painted duchess on her own hands, for a ruddy, healthy, firm-flesh'd country maid; and as for my part, that nature had done enough for me, to set me above owing the least favour to art; concluding withal, that for the instant occasion, there was no dress like an undress.

I thought my governess too good a judge of these matters not to be easily over-ruled by her: after which she went on preaching very pathetically the doctrine of passive obedience and not-resistance to all those arbitrary tastes of pleasure, which are by some styl'd the refinements, and by others the depravations of it; between whom it was not the business of a simple girl, who was to profit by pleasing, to decide, but to conform to. Whilst I was edifying by these wholesome lessons, tea was brought in, and the young ladies, returning, joined company with us.

After a great deal of mix'd chat, frolic and humour, one of them, observing that there would be a good deal of time on hand before the assembly-hour, proposed that each girl should entertain the company with that critical period of her personal history in which she first exchanged the maiden state for womanhood. The proposal was approv'd, with only one restriction of Mrs. Cole, that she, on account of her age, and I, on account of my titular maidenhead, should be excused, at least till I had undergone the forms of the house. This obtain'd me a dispensation, and the promotress of this amusement was desired to begin.

Her name was Emily; a girl fair to excess, and whose limbs were, if possible, too well made, since their plump fullness was rather to the prejudice of that delicate slimness requir'd by the nicer judges of beauty; her eyes were blue, and streamed inexpressible sweetness, and nothing could be prettier than her mouth and lips, which clos'd over a range of the evenest and whitest teeth. Thus she began:

"Neither my extraction, nor the most critical adventure of my life, is sublime enough to impeach me of any vanity in the advancement of the proposal you have approv'd of. My father and mother were, and for aught I know, are still, farmers in the country, not above forty miles from town: their barbarity to me, in favour of a son, on whom only they vouchsafed to bestow their tenderness, had a thousand times determined me to fly their house, and throw myself on the wide world; but, at length, an accident forc'd me on this desperate attempt at the age of fifteen. I had broken a china bowl, the pride and idol of both their hearts; and as an unmerciful beating was the least I had to depend on at their hands, in the silliness of those tender years I left the house, and, at all adventures, took the road to London. How my loss was resented I do not know, for till this instant I have not heard a syllable about them. My whole stock was too broad pieces of my grandmother's, a few shillings, silver shoe-buckles and a silver thimble. Thus equipp'd, with no more cloaths than the ordinary ones I had on my back, and frighten'd at every foot or noise I heard behind me, I hurried on; and I dare swear, walked a dozen miles before I stopped, through mere weariness and fatigue. At length I sat down on a stile, wept bitterly, and yet was still rather under increased impressions of fear on the account of my escape; which made dread, worse than death, the going back to face my unnatural parents. Refresh'd by this little repose, and relieved by my tears, I was proceeding onward, when I was overtaken by a sturdy country lad who was going to London to see what he could do for himself there, and, like me, had given his friends the slip. He could not be above seventeen, was ruddy, well featur'd enough, with uncombed flaxen hair, a little flapp'd hat, kersey frock, yarn stockings, in short, a perfect plough-boy. I saw him come whistling behind me, with a bundle tied to the end of a stick, his travelling equipage. We walk'd by one another for some time without speaking; at length we join'd company, and agreed to keep together till we got to our journey's end. What his designs or ideas were, I know not: the innocence of mine I can solemnly protest.

"As night drew on, it became us to look out for some inn or shelter; to which perplexity another was added, and that was, what we should say for ourselves, if we were question'd. After some puzzle, the young fellow started a proposal, which I thought the finest that could be; and what was that? why, that we should pass for husband and wife: I never once dream'd of consequences. We came presently, after having agreed on this notable expedient, to one of those hedge-accommodations for foot passengers, at the door do which stood an old crazy beldam, who seeing us trudge by, invited us to lodge there. Glad of any cover, we went in, and my fellow traveller, taking all upon him, call'd for what the house afforded, and we supped together as man and wife; which, considering our figures and ages, could not have passed on any one but such as any thing could pass on. But when bedtime came on, we had neither of us the courage to contradict out first account of ourselves;

and what was extremely pleasant, the young lad seem'd as perplex'd as I was, how to evade lying together, which was so natural for the state we had pretenced to. Whilst we were in this quandary, the landlady takes the candle and lights us to our apartment, through a long yard, at the end of which it stood, separate from the body of the house. Thus we suffer'd ourselves to be conducted, without saying a word in opposition to it; and there, in a wretched room, with a bed answerable, we were left to pass the night together, as a thing quite of course. For my part, I was so incredibly innocent as not even then to think much more harm of going to bed with the young man than with one of our dairy-wenches; nor had he, perhaps, any other notions than those of innocence, till such a fair occasion put them into his head.

"Before either of us undressed, however, he put out the candle; and the bitterness of the weather made it a kind of necessity for me to go into bed: slipping then my cloaths off, I crept under the bed-cloaths, where I found the young stripling already nestled, and the touch of his warm flesh rather pleas'd than alarm'd me. I was indeed too much disturbed with the novelty of my condition to be able to sleep; but then I had not the least thought of harm. But, oh! how powerful are the instincts of nature! how little is there wanting to set them in action! The young man, sliding his arm under my body, drew me gently towards him, as if to keep himself and me warmer; and the heat I felt from joining our breasts, kindled another that I had hitherto never felt, and was, even then, a stranger to the nature of. Emboldened, I suppose, by my easiness, he ventur'd to kiss me, and I insensibly returned it, without knowing the consequence of returning it; for, on this encouragement, he slipped his hand all down from my breast to that part of me where the sense of feeling is so exquisitely critical, as I then experienc'd by its instant taking fire upon the touch, and glowing with a strange tickling heat: there he pleas'd himself and me, by feeling, till, growing a little too bold, he hurt me, and made me complain. Then he took my hand, which he guided, not unwillingly on my side, between the twist of his closed thighs, which were extremely warm; there he lodged and pressed it, till raising it by degrees, he made me feel the proud distinction of his sex from mine. I was frighten'd at the novelty, and drew back my hand; yet, pressed and spurred on by sensations of a strange pleasure, I could not help asking him what that was for? He told me he would show me if I would let him; and, without waiting for my answer, which he prevented by stopping my mouth with kisses I was far from disrelishing, he got upon me, and inserting one of his thighs between mine, opened them so as to make way for himself, and fixed me to his purpose; whilst I was so much out of my usual sense, so subdu'd by the present power of a new one, that, between fear and desire, I lay utterly passive, till the piercing pain rous'd and made me cry out. But it was too late: he was too firm fix'd in the saddle for me to compass flinging him, with all the struggles I could use, some of which only served to further his point, and at length an irresistible thrust murdered at once my maidenhead, and almost me. I now lay a bleeding witness of the necessity impos'd on our sex, to gather the first honey off the thorns.

"But the pleasure rising as the pain subsided, I was soon reconciled to fresh trials, and before morning, nothing on earth could be dearer to me than this rifler of my virgin sweets: he was every thing to me now. How we agreed to join fortunes; how we came up to town together, where we lived some time, till necessity parted us, and drove me into this course of life, in which I had been long ago battered and torn to pieces before I came to this age, as much through my easiness, as through my inclination, had it not been for my finding refuge in this house: these are all circumstances which pass the mark I proposed, so that here my narrative ends."

In the order of our sitting, it was Harriet's turn to go on. Amongst all the beauties of our sex that I had before or have since seen, few indeed were the forms that could dispute excellence with her's; it was not delicate, but delicacy itself incarnate, such was the symmetry of her small but exactly fashion'd limbs. Her complexion, fair as it was, appeared yet more fair from the effect of two black eyes, the brilliancy of which gave her face more vivacity than belonged to the colour of it, which was only defended from paleness by a sweetly pleasing blush in her cheeks, that grew fainter and fainter, till at length it died away insensibly into the overbearing white. Then her miniature features join'd to finish the extreme sweetness of it, which was not belied by that of temper turned to indolence, languor, and the pleasures of love. Press'd to subscribe her contingent, she smiled, blushed a little, and thus complied with our desires:

"My father was neither better nor worse than a miller near the city of York; and both he and my mother dying whilst I was an infant, I fell under the care of a widow and childless aunt, housekeeper to my lord N——, at his seat in the county of ——, where she brought me up with all imaginable tenderness. I was not seventeen, as I am not now eighteen, before I had, on account of my person purely (for fortune I had notoriously none), several advantageous proposals; but whether nature was slow in making me sensible in her favourite passion, or that I had not seen any of the other sex who had stirr'd up the least emotion or curiosity to be better acquainted with it, I had, till that age, preserv'd a perfect innocence, even of thought: whilst my fears of I did not well know what, made me no more desirous of marrying than of dying. My aunt, good woman, favoured my timorousness, which she look'd on as childish affection, that her own experience might probably assure her would wear off in time, and gave my suitors proper answers for me.

"The family had not been down at that seat for years, so that it was neglected, and committed entirely to my aunt, and two old domestics to take care of it. Thus I had the full range of a spacious lonely house and gardens, situate at about half a mile distance form any other habitation, except, perhaps, a straggling cottage or so.

"Here, in tranquillity and innocence, I grew up without any memorable accident, till one fatal day I had, as I had often done before, left my aunt fast asleep, and secure for some hours, after dinner; and resorting to a kind of ancient summer-house, at some distance from the house, I carried my work with me, and sat over a rivulet, which its door and window fac'd upon. Here I fell into a gentle breathing slumber, which stole upon my senses, as they fainted under the excessive heat of the season at that hour; a cane couch, with my work-basket for a pillow, were all the conveniencies of my short repose; for I was soon awaked and alarmed by a flounce, and the noise of splashing in the water. I got up to see what was the matter; and what indeed should it be but the son of a neighbouring gentleman, as I afterwards found (for I had never seen him before), who had strayed that way with his gun, and heated by his sport, and the sultriness of the day, had been tempted by the freshness of the clear stream; so that presently stripping, he jump'd into it on the other side, which bordered on a wood, some trees whereof, inclined down to the water, form'd a pleasing shady recess, commodious to undress and leave his clothes under.

"My first emotions at the sight of this youth, naked in the water, were, with all imaginable respect to truth, those of surprise and fear; and, in course, I should immediately have run out, had not my modesty, fatally for itself, interposed the objection of the door and window being so situated that it was scarce possible to get out, and make my way along the bank to the house, without his seeing me: which I could not bear the thought of, so much ashamed and confounded was I at having seen him. Condemn'd then to stay till his departure should release me, I was greatly embarrassed how to dispose of myself: I kept some time betwixt terror and modesty, even from looking through the window, which being an old-fashion'd casement, without any light behind me, could hardly betray any one's being there to him from within; then the door was so secure, that without violence, or my own consent, there was no opening it from without.

"But now, by my own experience, I found it too true that objects which affright us, when we cannot get from them, draw out eyes as forcibly as those that please us. I could not long withstand that nameless impulse, which, without any desire of this novel sight, compelled me towards it; embolden'd too by my certainty of being at once unseen and safe, I ventur'd by degrees to cast my eyes on an object so terrible and alarming to my virgin modesty as a naked man. But as I snatched a look, the first gleam that struck me was in general the dewy lustre of the whitest skin imaginable, which the sun playing upon made the reflection of it perfectly beamy. His face, in the confusion I was in, I could not well distinguish the lineaments of, any farther than that there was a great deal of youth and freshness in it. The frolic and various play of all his polish'd limbs, as they appeared above the surface, in the course of his swimming or wantoning with the water, amus'd and insensibly delighted me: sometimes he lay motionless, on his back, waterborne, and dragging after him a fine head of hair, that, floating, swept the stream in a bush of black curls. Then the over-flowing water would make a separation between his breast and glossy white belly; at the bottom of which I could not escape observing so remarkable a distinction as a black mossy tuft, out of which appeared to emerge a round, softish, limber, white something, that played every way, with ever the least motion or whirling eddy. I cannot say but that part chiefly, by a kind of natural

THE SCARLET LIBRARY

instinct, attracted, detain'd, captivated my attention: it was out of the power of all my modesty to command my eye away from it; and seeing nothing so very dreadful in its appearance, I insensibly lock'd away all my fears: but as fast as they gave way, new desires and strange wishes took place, and I melted as I gazed. The fire of nature, that had so long lain dormant or conceal'd, began to break out, and made me feel my sex the first time. He had now changed his posture, and swam prone on his belly, striking out with his legs and arms, finer modell'd than which could not have been cast, whilst his floating locks played over a neck and shoulders whose whiteness they delightfully set off. Then the luxuriant swell of flesh that rose form the small of his back, and terminated its double cope at where the thighs are sent off, perfectly dazzled one with its watery glistening gloss.

"By this time I was so affected by this inward involution of sentiments, so soften'd by this sight, that now, betrayed into a sudden transition from extreme fears to extreme desires, I found these last so strong upon me, the heat of the weather too perhaps conspiring to exalt their rage, that nature almost fainted under them. Not that I so much as knew precisely what was wanting to me: my only thought was that so sweet a creature as this youth seemed to me could only make me happy; but then, the little likelihood there was of compassing an acquaintance with him, or perhaps of ever seeing him again, dash'd my desires, and turn'd them into torments. I was still gazing, with all the powers of my sight, on this bewitching object, when, in an instant, down he went. I had heard of such things as a cramp seizing on even the best swimmers, and occasioning their being drowned; and imagining this so sudden eclipse to be owing to it, the inconceivable fondness this unknown lad had given birth to distracted me with the most killing terrors; insomuch, that my concern giving the wings, I flew to the door, open'd it, ran down to the canal, guided thither by the madness of my fears for him, and the intense desire of being an instrument to save him, though I was ignorant how, or by what means to effect it: but was it for fears, and a passion so sudden as mine, to reason? All this took up scarce the space of a few moments. I had then just life enough to reach the green borders of the waterpiece, where wildly looking round for the young man, and missing him still, my fright and concern sunk me down in a deep swoon, which must have lasted me some time; for I did not come to myself till I was rous'd out of it by a sense of pain that pierced me to the vitals, and awaked me to the most surprising circumstance of finding myself not only in the arms of this very same young gentleman I had been so solicitous to save, but taken at such an advantage in my unresisting condition that he had actually completed his entrance into me so far, that weakened as I was by all the preceding conflicts of mind I had suffer'd, and struck dumb by the violence of my surprise, I had neither the power to cry out nor the strength to disengage myself from his strenuous embraces, before, urging his point, he had forced his way and completely triumphed over my virginity, as he might now as well see by the streams of blood that follow'd his drawing out, as he had felt by the difficulties he had met with consummating his penetration. But the sight of the blood, and the sense of my condition, had (as he told me afterwards), since the ungovernable rage of his passion was somewhat appeas'd, now wrought so far on him that at all risks, even of the worst consequences, he could not find in his heart to leave me, and make off, which he might easily have done. I still lay all descompos'd in bleeding ruin, palpitating, speechless, unable to get off, and frightened, and fluttering like a poor wounded partridge, and ready to faint away again at the sense of what had befallen me. The young gentleman was by me, kneeling, kissing my hand, and with tears in his eyes beseeching me to forgive him, and offering all the reparation in his power. It is certain that could I, at the instant of regaining my senses, have called out, or taken the bloodiest revenge, I would not have stuck at it: the violation was attended too with such aggravating circumstances, though he was ignorant of them, since it was to my concern for the preservation of his life that I owed my ruin.

"But how quick is the shift of passions from one extreme to another! and how little are they acquainted with the human heart who dispute it! I could not see this amiable criminal, so suddenly the first object of my love, and as suddenly of my just hate, on his knees, bedewing my hand with his tears, without relenting. He was still stark-naked, but my modesty had been already too much wounded, in essentials, to be so much shocked as I should have otherwise been with appearances only; in short, my anger ebbed so fast, and the tide of love return'd so strong upon me, that I felt it a point of my own happiness to forgive him. The reproaches I made him were murmur'd in so soft a tone, my eyes met his with such glances, expressing more languor than resentment, that he could not but presume his forgiveness was at no desperate distance; but still he would not quit his posture of submission, till I had pronounced his pardon in form; which after the most fervent entreaties, protestations, and promises, I had not the power to withhold. On which, with the utmost marks of a fear of again offending, he ventured to kiss my lips, which I neither declined nor resented; but on my mild expostulations with him upon the barbarity of his treatment, he explain'd the mystery of my ruin, if not entirely to the clearance, at least much to the alleviation of his guilt, in the eyes of a judge so partial in his favour as I was grown.

"Its seems that the circumstance of his going down, or sinking, which in my extreme ignorance I had mistaken for something very fatal, was no other than a trick of diving which I had not ever heard, or at least attended to, the mention of:

and he was so long-breath'd at it, that in the few moments in which I ran out to save him, he had not yet emerged, before I fell into the swoon, in which, as he rose, seeing me extended on the bank, his first idea was that some young woman was upon some design of frolic or diversion with him, for he knew I could not have fallen a-sleep there without his having seen me before: agreeably to which notion he had ventured to approach, and finding me without sign of life, and still perplex'd as he was what to think of the adventure, he took me in his arms at all hazards, and carried me into the summer-house, of which he observed the door open: there he laid me down on the couch, and tried, as he protested in good faith, by several means to bring me to myself again, till fired, as he said, beyond all bearing by the sight and touch of several parts of me which were unguardedly exposed to him, he could no longer govern his passion; and the less, as he was not quite sure that his first idea of this swoon being a feint was not the very truth of the case: seduced then by this flattering notion, and overcome by the present, as he styled them, superhuman temptations, combined with the solitude and seeming security of the attempt, he was not enough his own master not to make it. Leaving me then just only whilst he fastened the door, he returned with redoubled eagerness to his prey: when, finding me still entranced, he ventured to place me as he pleased, whilst I felt, no more than the dead, what he was about, till the pain he put me to roused me just in time enough to be witness of a triumph I was not able to defeat, and now scarce regretted: for as he talked, the tone of his voice sounded, methought, so sweetly in my ears, the sensible nearness of so new and interesting an object to me wrought so powerfully upon me, that, in the rising perception of things in a new and pleasing light, I lost all sense of the past injury. The young gentleman soon discern'd the symptoms of a reconciliation in my softened looks, and hastening to receive the seal of it from my lips,

press'd them tenderly to pass his pardon in the return of a kiss so melting fiery, that the impression of it being carried to my heart, and thence to my new-discover'd sphere of Venus, I was melted into a softness that could refuse him nothing. When now he managed his caresses and endearments so artfully as to insinuate the most soothing consolations for the past pain and the most pleasing expectations of future pleasure, but whilst mere modesty kept my eyes from seeing his and rather declined them, I had a glimpse of that instrument of the mischief which was now, obviously even to me, who had scarce had snatches of a comparative observation of it, resuming its capacity to renew it, and grew greatly alarming with its increase of size, as he bore it no doubt designedly, hard and stiff against one of my hands carelessly dropt; but then he employ'd such tender prefacing, such winning progressions, that my returning passion of desire being now so strongly prompted by the engaging circumstances of the sight and incendiary touch of his naked glowing beauties, I yielded at length at the force of the present impressions, and he obtained of my tacit blushing consent all the gratifications of pleasure left in the power of my poor person to bestow, after he had cropt its richest flower, during my suspension of life and abilities to guard it.

"Here, according to the rule laid down, I should stop; but I am so much in motion, that I could not if I would. I shall only add, however, that I got home without the least discovery, or suspicion of what had happened. I met my young ravisher several times after, whom I now passionately lov'd and who, tho' not of age to claim a small but independent fortune, would have married me; but as the accidents that prevented it, and their consequences which threw me on the publick, contain matters too moving and serious to introduce at present, I cut short here."

Louisa, the brunette whom I mentioned at first, now took her turn to treat the company with her history. I have already hinted to you the graces of her person, than which nothing could be more exquisitely touching; I repeat touching, as a just distinction from striking, which is ever a less lasting effect, and more generally belongs to the fair complexions: but leaving that decision to every one's taste, I proceed to give you Louisa's narrative as follows:

"According to practical maxims of life, I ought to boast of my birth, since I owe it to pure love, without marriage; but this I know, it was scarce possible to inherit a stronger propensity to that cause of my being than I did. I was the rare production of the first essay of a journeyman cabinet-maker on his master's maid: the consequence of which was a big belly, and the loss of a place. He was not in circumstances to do much for her; and yet, after all this blemish, she found means, after she had dropt her burthen and disposed of me to a poor relation's in the country, to repair it by marrying a pastry-cook here in London, in thriving business; on whom she soon, under favour of the complete ascendant he had given her over him, passed me for a child she had by her first husband. I had, on that footing, been taken home, and was not six years old when this stepfather died and left my mother in tolerable circumstances, and without any children by him. As to my natural father, he had betaken himself to the sea; where, when the truth of things came out, I was told that he died, not immensely rich you may think, since he was no more than a common sailor. As I grew up, under the eyes of my mother, who kept on the business, I could not but see, in her severe watchfulness, the marks of a slip which she did not care should be hereditary, but we no more choose our passions than our features or complexion, and the bent of mine was so strong to the forbidden pleasure, that it got the better, at length, of all her care and precaution. I was scarce twelve years old before that part which she wanted so much to keep out of harm's way made me feel its impatience to be taken notice of, and come into play: already had it put forth the signs of forwardness in the sprout of a soft down over it, which had often flatter'd, and I might also say, grown under my constant touch and visitation, so pleas'd was I with what I took to be a kind of title to womanhood, that state I pin'd to be entr'd of, for the pleasures I conceiv'd were annexed to it; and now the growing importance of that part to me, and the new sensations in it, demolish'd at once all my girlish playthings and amusements. Nature now pointed me strongly to more solid diversions, while all the stings of desire settled so fiercely in that little centre of them, that I could not mistake the spot I wanted a playfellow in. I now shunn'd all company in which there was no hopes of coming at the object of my longings, and used to shut myself up, to indulge in solitude some tender meditation on the pleasures I strongly perceiv'd the overture of, in feeling and examining what nature assur'd me must be the chosen avenue, the gates for unknown bliss to enter at, that I panted after.

"But these meditations only increas'd my disorder, and blew the fire that consumed me. I was yet worse when, yielding at length to the insupportable irritations of the little fairy charm that tormented me, I seiz'd it with my fingers, teasing it to no end. Sometimes, in the furious excitations of desire, I threw myself on the bed, spread my thighs abroad, and lay as it were expecting the longed-for relief, till finding my illusion, I shut and squeez'd them together again, burning and fretting. In short, this dev'lish thing, with its impetuous girds and itching fires, led me such a life that I could neither night nor day be at peace with it or myself. In time, however, I thought I had gained a prodigious prize, when figuring to myself that my fingers were something of the shape of what I pined for, I worked my way in for one of them with great agitation and delight; yet not without pain too did I deflower myself as far as it could reach; proceeding with such a fury of passion, in this solitary and last shift of pleasure, as extended me at length breathless on the bed in an amorous melting trance.

"But frequency of use dulling the sensation, I soon began to perceive that this work was but a paltry shallow expedient that went but a little way to relieve me, and rather rais'd more flame than its dry and insignificant titillation could rightly appease.

"Man alone, I almost instinctively knew, as well as by what I had industriously picked up at weddings and christenings, was possess'd of the only remedy that could reduce this rebellious disorder; but watch'd and overlook'd as I was, how to come at it was the point, and that, to all appearance, an invincible one; not that I did not rack my brains and invention how at once to elude my mother's vigilance, and procure myself the satisfaction of my impetuous curiosity and longings for this mighty and untasted pleasure. At length, however, a singular chance did at once the work of a long course of alertness. One day that we had dined at an acquaintance's over the way, together with a gentlewoman-lodger that occupied the first floor of our house, there started an indispensable necessity for my mother's going down to Greenwich to accompany her: the party was settled, when I do not know what genius whispered me to plead a headache, which I certainly had not, against my being included in a jaunt that I had not the least relish for. The pretext however passed, and my mother, with much reluctance, prevailed with herself to go without me; but took particular care to see me safe home, where she consign'd me into the hands of an old trusty maid-servant, who served in the shop, for we had not a male creature in the house.

"As soon as she was gone, I told the maid I would go up and lie down on our lodger's bed, mine not being made, with a charge to her at the same time not to disturb me, as it was only rest I wanted. This injunction probably prov'd of eminent service to me. As soon as I was got into the bedchamber, I unlaced my stays, and threw myself on the outside of the bed-cloaths, in all the loosest undress. Here I gave myself up to the old insipid privy shifts of my self-viewing, self-touching, self-enjoying, in fine, to all the means of self-knowledge I could devise, in search of the pleasure that fled before me, and tantalized with that unknown something that was out of my reach; thus all only serv'd to enflame myself, and to provoke violently my desires, whilst the one thing needful to their satisfaction was not at hand, and I could have bit my fingers, for representing it so ill. After then wearying and fatiguing myself with grasping shadows, whilst that most sensible part of me disdain'd to content itself with less than realities, the strong yearnings, the urgent struggles of nature towards the melting relief, and the extreme self-agitations I had used to come at it, had wearied and thrown me into a kind of unquiet sleep: for, if I tossed and threw about my limbs in proportion to the distraction of my dreams, as I had reason to believe I did, a bystander could not have help'd seeing all for love. And one there was it seems; for waking out of my very short slumber, I found my hand lock'd in that of a young man, who was kneeling at my bed-side, and begging my pardon for his boldness: but that being a son to the lady to whom this bedchamber, he knew, belonged, he had slipp'd by the servant of the shop, as he supposed, unperceiv'd, when finding me asleep, his first ideas were to withdraw; but that he had been fix'd and detain'd there by a power he could better account for than resist.

"What shall I say? my emotions of fear and surprise were instantly subdued by those of the pleasure I bespoke in great presence of mind from the turn this adventure might take. He seem'd to me no other than a pitying angel, dropt out of the clouds: for he was young and perfectly handsome, which was more than even I had asked for; man, in general, being all that my utmost desires had pointed at. I thought then I could not put too much encouragement into my eyes and voice; I regretted no leading advances; no matter for his after-opinion of my forwardness, so it might bring him to the point of answering my pressing demands of present case; it was not now with his thoughts, but his actions, that my business immediately lay. I rais'd then my head, and told him, in a soft tone that tended to prescribe the same key to him, that his mamma was gone out and would not return till late at night: which I thought no bad hint; but as it prov'd, I had nothing of a novice to deal with. The impressions I had made on him from the discoveries I had betrayed of my person in the disordered motions of it, during his view of me asleep, had, as he afterwards told me, so fix'd and charmingly prepar'd him, that, had I known his dispositions, I had more to hope from his violence than to fear from his respect; and even less than the extreme tenderness which I threw into my voice and eyes, would have served to encourage him to make the most of the opportunity. Finding then that his kisses, imprinted on my hand, were taken as tamely as he could wish, he rose to my lips; and glewing his to them, made me so faint with over-coming joy and pleasure that I fell back, and he with me, in course, on the bed, upon which I had, by insensibly shifting

FANNY HILL VOL II

from the side to near the middle, invitingly made room for him. He is now lain down by me, and the minutes being too precious to consume in untimely ceremony, or dalliance, my youth proceeds immediately to those extremities, which all my looks, flushing and palpitations had assured him he might attempt without the fear of repulse: those rogues, the men, read us admirably on these occasions. I lay then at length panting for the imminent attack, with wishes far beyond my fears, and for which it was scarce possible for a girl, barely thirteen, but all and well grown, to have better dispositions. He threw up my petticoat and shift, whilst my thighs were, by an instinct of nature, unfolded to their best; and my desires had so thoroughly destroy'd all modesty in me, that even their being now naked and all laid open to him, was part of the prelude that pleasure deepen'd my blushes at, more than shame. But when his hand, and touches, naturally attracted to their centre, made me feel all their wantonness and warmth in, and round it, oh! how immensely different a sense of things did I perceive there, than when under my own insipid handling! And now his waistcoat was unbuttoned, and the confinement of the breeches burst through, when out started to view the amazing, pleasing object of all my wishes, all my dreams, all my love, the king member indeed! I gaz'd at, I devoured it, at length and breadth, with my eyes intently directed to it, till his getting upon me, and placing it between my thighs, took from me the enjoyment of its sight, to give me a far more grateful one in its touch, in that part where its touch is so exquisitely affecting. Applying it then to the minute opening, for such at that age it certainly was, I met with too much good will, I felt with too great a rapture of pleasure the first insertion of it, to heed much the pain that followed: I thought nothing too dear to pay for this the richest treat of the senses; so that, split up, torn, bleeding, mangled, I was still superiorly pleas'd, and hugg'd the author of all this delicious ruin. But when, soon after, he made his second attack, sore as every thing was, the smart was soon put away by the sovereign cordial; all my soft complainings were silenc'd, and the pain melting fast away into pleasure. I abandon'd myself over to all its transports, and gave it the full possession of my whole body and soul; for now all thought was at an end with me; I lived but in what I felt only. And who could describe those feelings, those agitations, yet exalted by the charm of their novelty and surprise? when that part of me which had so long hunger'd for the dear morsel that now so delightfully crammed it, forc'd all my vital sensations to fix their home there, during the stay of my beloved guest; who too soon paid me for his hearty welcome in a dissolvent, richer far than that I have heard of some queen treating her paramour with, in liquify'd pearl, and ravishingly pour'd into me, where, now myself too much melted to give it a dry reception, I hail'd it with the warmest confluence on my side, amidst all those extatic raptures, not unfamiliar I presume to this good company! Thus, however, I arrived at the very top of all my wishes, by an accident unexpected indeed, but not so wonderful; for this young gentleman was just arriv'd in town from college, and came familiarly to his mother at her apartment, where he had once before been, though by mere chance. I had not seen him: so that we knew one another by hear-say only; and finding me stretched on his mother's bed, he readily concluded, from her description who it was. The rest you know.

"This affair had however no ruinous consequences, the young

gentleman escaping then, and many more times undiscover'd. But the warmth of my constitution, that made the pleasures of love a kind of necessary of life to me, having betray'd me into indiscretions fatal to my private fortune, I fell at length to the publick; from which, it is probable, I might have met with the worst of ruin if my better fate had not thrown me into this safe and agreeable refuge."

Here Louisa ended; and these little histories having brought the time for the girls to retire, and to prepare for the revels of the evening, I staid with Mrs. Cole till Emily came and told us the company was met, and waited for us.

PART VII

On the landing-place of the first pair of stairs, we were met by a young gentleman, extremely well dress'd, and a very pretty figure, to whom I was to be indebted for the first essay of the pleasures of the house. He saluted me with great gallantry, and handed me into the drawing room, the floor of which was overspread with a Turkey carpet, and all its furniture voluptuously adapted to every demand of the most study'd luxury; now too it was, by means of a profuse illumination, enliven'd by a light scarce inferior, and perhaps more favourable to joy, more tenderly pleasing, than that of broad sun-shine.

On my entrance into the room, I had the satisfaction to hear a buzz of approbation run through the whole company which now consisted of four gentlemen, including my particular (this was the cant-term of the house for one's gallant for the time), the three young women, in a neat flowing dishabille, the mistress of the academy, and myself. I was welcomed and saluted by a kiss all round, in which, however, it was easy to discover, in the superior warmth of that of the men, the distinction of the sexes.

Aw'd and confounded as I was at seeing myself surrounded, caress'd, and made court to by so many strangers, I could not immediately familiarize myself to all that air of gaiety and joy which dictated their compliments, and animated their caresses.

They assur'd me that I was so perfectly to their taste as to have but one fault against me, which I might easily be cur'd of, and that was my modesty: this, they observ'd, might pass for a beauty the more with those who wanted it for a heightener; but their maxim was, that it was an impertinent mixture, and dash'd the cup so as to spoil the sincere draught of pleasure; they consider'd it accordingly as their mortal enemy, and gave it no quarter wherever they met with it. This was a prologue not unworthy of the revels that ensu'd.

In the midst of all the frolic and wantonnesses, which this joyous band had presently, and all naturally, run into, an elegant supper was serv'd in, and we sat down to it, my spark-elect placing himself next to me, and the other couples without order or ceremony. The delicate cheer and good wine soon banish'd all reserve; the conversation grew as lively as could be wished, without taking too loose a turn: these professors of pleasure knew too well, to stale impressions of it, or evaporate the imagination in words, before the time of action. Kisses however were snatch'd at times, or where a handkerchief round the neck interpos'd its feeble barrier, it was not extremely respected: the hands of the men went to work with their usual petulance, till the provocations on both sides rose to such a pitch that my particular's proposal for beginning the country-dances was received with instant assent: for, as he laughingly added, he fancied the instruments were in tune. This was a signal for preparation, that the complaisant Mrs. Cole, who understood life, took for her cue of disappearing; no longer so fit for personal service herself, and content with having settled the order of battle, she left us the field, to fight it out at discretion.

As soon as she was gone, the table was remov'd form the middle, and became a side-board; a couch was brought into its place, of which when I whisperingly inquired the reason, of my particular, he told me that as it was chiefly on my account that this convention was met, the parties intended at once to humour their taste of variety in pleasures, and by an open publick enjoyment, to see me broke of any taint of reserve or modesty, which they look'd on as the poison of joy; that though they occasionally preached pleasure, and lived up to the text, they did not enthusiastically set up for missionaries, and only indulg'd themselves in the delights of a practical instruction of all the pretty women they lik'd well enough to bestow it upon, and who fell properly in the way of it; but that as such a proposal might be too violent, too shocking for a young beginner, the old standers were to set an example, which he hoped I would not be averse to follow, since it was to him I was devolv'd in favour of the first experiment; but that still I was perfectly at my liberty to refuse the party, which being in its nature one of pleasure, suppos'd an exclusion of all force or constraint.

My countenance expressed, no doubt, my surprise as my silence did my acquiescence. I was now embarked, and thoroughly determined on any voyage the company would take me on. The first that stood up, to open the ball, were a cornet of horse, and that sweetest of olive-beauties, the soft and amorous Louisa. He led her to the couch "nothing loth," on which he gave her the fall, and extended her at her length with an air of roughness and vigour, relishing high of amorous eagerness and impatience. The girl, spreading herself to the best advantage, with her head upon the pillow, was so concentred in what she was about, that our presence seemed the least of her care and concern. Her petticoats, thrown up with her shift, discovered to the company the finest turn'd legs and thighs that could be imagined, and in broad display, that gave us a full view of that delicious cleft of flesh into which the pleasing hair-grown mount over it, parted and presented a most inviting entrance between two close-hedges, delicately soft and pouting. Her gallant was now ready, having disencumber'd himself from his cloaths, overloaded with lace, and presently, his shirt removed, shew'd us his forces in high plight, bandied and ready for action. But giving us no time to consider the dimensions, he threw himself instantly over his charming antagonist, who receiv'd him as he pushed at once dead at mark like a heroine, without flinching; for surely never was girl constitutionally

truer to the taste of joy, or sincerer in the expressions of its sensations, than she was: we could observe pleasure lighten in her eyes, as he introduc'd his plenipotentiary instrument into her; till, at length, having indulg'd her to its utmost reach, its irritations grew so violent, and gave her the spurs so furiously, that collected within herself, and lost to everything but the enjoyment of her favourite feelings, she retorted his thrusts with a just concert of springy heaves, keeping time so exactly with the most pathetic sighs, that one might have number'd the strokes in agitation by their distinct murmurs, whilst her active limbs kept wreathing and intertwisting with his, in convulsive folds: then the turtle-billing kisses, and the poignant painless lovebites, which they both exchang'd in a rage of delight, all conspiring towards the melting period. It soon came on when Louisa, in the ravings of her pleasure-frenzy, impotent of all restraint, cried out: "Oh Sir! . . . Good Sir! . . . pray do not spare me! ah! ah! . . ." All her accents now faltering into heart-fetched sighs, she clos'd her eyes in the sweet death, in the instant of which she was embalm'd by an injection, of which we could easily see the signs in the quiet, dying, languid posture of her late so furious driver, who was stopp'd of a sudden, breathing short, panting, and, for the time, giving up the spirit of pleasure. As soon as he was dismounted, Louisa sprung up, shook her petticoats, and running up to me, gave me a kiss and drew me to the side-board, to which she was herself handed by her gallant, where they made me pledge them in a glass of wine, and toast a droll health of Louisa's proposal in high frolic.

By this time the second couple was ready to enter the lists: which were a young baronet, and that delicatest of charmers, the winning, tender Harriet. My gentle esquire came to acquaint me with it, and brought me back to the scene of action.

And, surely, never did one of her profession accompany her dispositions for the bare-faced part she was engaged to play with such a peculiar grace of sweetness, modesty and yielding coyness, as she did. All her air and motions breath'd only unreserv'd, unlimited complaisance without the least mixture of impudence, or prostitution. But what was yet more surprising, her spark-elect, in the midst of the dissolution of a publick open enjoyment, doted on her to distraction, and had, by dint of love and sentiments, touched her heart, tho' for a while the restraint of their engagement to the house laid him under a kind of necessity of complying with an institution which himself had had the greatest share in establishing.

Harriet was then led to the vacant couch by her gallant, blushing as she look'd at me, and with eyes made to justify any thing, tenderly bespeaking of me the most favourable construction of the step she was thus irresistibly drawn into.

Her lover, for such he was, sat her down at the foot of the couch, and passing his arm round her neck, preluded with a kiss fervently applied to her lips, that visibly gave her life and spirit to go thro' with the scene; and as he kiss'd, he gently inclined her head, till it fell back on a pillow disposed to receive it, and leaning himself down all the way with her, at once countenanc'd and endear'd her fall to her. There, as if he had guess'd our wishes, or meant to gratify at once his pleasure and his pride, in being the master, by the title of present possession, of beauties delicate beyond imagination, he discovered her breasts to his own touch, and our common view; but oh! what delicious manuals of love devotion! how inimitable fine moulded! small, round, firm, and excellently white: the grain of their skin, so soothing, so flattering to the touch! and their nipples, that crown'd them, the sweetest buds of beauty. When he had feasted his eyes with the touch and perusal, feasted his lips with kisses of the highest relish, imprinted on those all-delicious twin orbs, the proceeded downwards.

Her legs still kept the ground; and now, with the tenderest attention not to shock or alarm her too suddenly, he, by degrees, rather stole than rolled up her petticoats; at which, as if a signal had been given, Louisa and Emily took hold of her legs, in pure wantonness, and, in ease to her, kept them stretched wide abroad. Then lay exposed, or, to speak more properly, display'd the greatest parade in nature of female charms. The whole company, who, except myself, had often seen them, seemed as much dazzled, surpriz'd and delighted, as any one could be who had now beheld them for the first time. Beauties so excessive could not but enjoy the privileges of eternal novelty. Her thighs were so exquisitely fashioned, that either more in, or more out of flesh than they were, they would have declined from that point of perfection they presented. But what infinitely enrich'd and adorn'd them, was the sweet intersection formed, where they met, at the bottom of the smoothest, roundest, whitest belly, by that central furrow which nature had sunk there, between, the soft relieve of two pouting ridges, and which in this was in perfect symmetry of delicacy and miniature with the rest of her frame. No! nothing in nature could be of a beautifuller cut; then, the dark umbrage of the downy spring-moss that over-arched it bestowed, on the luxury of the landscape, a touching warmth, a tender finishing, beyond the expression of words, or even the paint of thought. Her truly enamour'd gallant, who had stood absorbed and engrossed by the pleasure of the sight long enough to afford us time to feast ours (no fear of glutting!) addressed himself at length to the materials of enjoyment, and lifting the linen veil that hung between us and his master member of the revels, exhibited one whose eminent size proclaimed the owner a true woman's hero. He was, besides, in every other respect an accomplish'd gentleman, and in the bloom and vigour of youth. Standing then between Harriet's legs, which were supported by her

FANNY HILL VOL II

two companions at their widest extension, with one hand he gently disclosed the lips of that luscious mouth of nature, whilst with the other, he stooped his mighty machine to its lure, from the height of his stiff stand-up towards his belly; the lips, kept open by his fingers, received its broad shelving head of coral hue: and when he had nestled it in, he hovered there a little, and the girls then deliver'd over to his hips the agreeable office of supporting her thighs; and now, as if meant to spin out his pleasure, and give it the more play for its life, he passed up his instrument so slow that we lost sight of it inch by inch, till at length it was wholly taken into the soft laboratory of love, and the mossy mounts of each fairly met together. In the mean time, we could plainly mark the prodigious effect the progressions of this delightful energy wrought in this delicious girl, gradually heightening her beauty as they heightened her pleasure. Her countenance and whole frame grew more animated; the faint blush of her cheeks, gaining ground on the white, deepened into a florid vivid vermilion glow, her naturally brilliant eyes now sparkled with ten-fold lustre; her languor was vanish'd, and she appeared, quick spirited, and alive all over. He now fixed, nailed, this tender creature with his home-driven wedge, so that she lay passive by force, and unable to stir, till beginning to play a strain of arms against this vein of delicacy, as he urged the to-and-fro confriction, he awaken'd, rous'd, and touch'd her so to the heart, that unable to contain herself, she could not but reply to his motions as briskly as her nicety of frame would admit of, till the raging stings of the pleasure rising towards the point, made her wild with the intolerable sensations of it, and she now threw her legs and arms about at random, as she lay lost in the sweet transport; which on his side declared itself by quicker, eager thrusts, convulsive gasps, burning sighs, swift laborious breathings, eyes darting humid fires: all faithful tokens of the imminent approaches of the last gasp of joy. It came on at length: the baronet led the ecstasy, which she critically joined in, as she felt the melting symptoms from him, in the nick of which glewing more ardently than ever his lips to hers, he shewed all the signs of that agony of bliss being strong upon him, in which he gave her the finishing titillation; inly thrill'd with which, we saw plainly that she answered it down with all effusion of spirit and matter she was mistress of, whilst a general soft shudder ran through all her limbs, which she gave a stretch-out of, and lay motionless, breathless, dying with dear delight; and in the height of its expression, shewing, through the nearly closed lids of her eyes, just the edges of their black, the rest being rolled strongly upwards in their ecstasy; then her sweet mouth appear'd languishingly open, with the tip of her tongue leaning negligently towards the lower range of her white teeth, whilst the natural ruby colour of her lips glowed with heightened life. Was not this a subject to dwell upon? And accordingly her lover still kept on her, with an abiding delectation, till compressed, squeezed and distilled to the last drop, he took leave with one fervent kiss, expressing satisfy'd desires, but unextinguish'd love.

As soon as he was off, I ran to her, and sitting down on the couch by her, rais'd her head, which she declin'd gently, and hung on my bosom, to hide her blushes and confusion at what had pass'd, till by degrees she recomposed herself and accepted of a restorative glass of wine from my spark, who had left me to fetch it her, whilst her own was re-adjusting his affairs and buttoning up; after which he led her, leaning languishingly upon him, to our stand of view round the couch.

And now Emily's partner had taken her out for her share in the dance, when this transcendently fair and sweet tempered creature readily stood up; and if a complexion to put the rose and lily out of countenance, extreme pretty features, and that florid health and bloom for which the country-girls are so lovely, might pass her for a beauty, this she certainly was, and one of the most striking of the fair ones.

Her gallant began first, as she stood, to disengage her breasts, and restore them to the liberty of nature, from the easy confinement of no more than a pair of jumps; but on their coming out to view, we thought a new light was added to the room, so superiourly shining was their whiteness; then they rose in so happy a swell as to compose her a well-formed fullness of bosom, that had such an effect on the eye as to seem flesh hardening into marble, of which it emulated the polished gloss, and far surpassed even the whitest, in the life and lustre of its colours, white veined with blue. Refrain who could from such provoking enticements to it in reach? He touched her breasts, first lightly, when the glossy smoothness of the skin eluded his hand, and made it slip along the surface; he press'd them, and the springy flesh that filled them thus pitted by force, rose again reboundingly with his hand, and on the instant effac'd the pressure: and alike indeed was the consistence of all those parts of her body throughout, where the fullness of flesh compacts and constitutes all that fine firmness which the touch is so highly attach'd to. When he had thus largely pleased himself with this branch of dalliance and delight, he truss'd up her petticoat and shift in a wisp to her waist, where being tuck'd in, she stood fairly naked on every side; a blush at this overspread her lovely face, and her eyes down cast to the ground seemed to be for quarter, when she had so great a right to triumph in all the treasures of youth and beauty that she now so victoriously display'd. Her legs were perfectly well shaped and her thighs, which she kept pretty close, shewed so white, so round, so substantial and abounding in firm flesh, that nothing could offer a stronger recommendation to the luxury of the touch, which he accordingly did not fail to indulge himself in. Then gently removing her hand, which in the first emotion of natural modesty she had carried thither, he gave us rather a glimpse than a view of that soft narrow chink running its little length downwards and hiding the remains of it between her thighs; but plain was to be seen the fringe of light-brown curls, in beauteous growth over it, that with their silky gloss created a pleasing variety from the surrounding white, whose lustre too, their gentle embrowning shade, considerably raised. Her spark then endeavoured, as she stood, by disclosing her thighs, to gain us a completer sight of that central charm of attraction, but not obtaining it so conveniently in that attitude, he led her to the foot of the couch, and bringing to it one of the pillows, gently inclin'd her head down, so that as she leaned with it over her crossed hands, straddling with her thighs wide spread, and jutting her body out, she presented a full back view of her person, naked to the waist. Her posteriours, plump, smooth, and prominent, form'd luxuriant tracts of animated snow, that splendidly filled the eye, till it was commanded down the parting or separation of those exquisitely white cliffs, by their narrow vale, and was there stopt, and attracted by the embowered bottom-cavity, that terminated this delightful vista and stood moderately gaping from the influence of her bended posture, so that the agreeable, interior red of the sides of the orifice came into view, and with respect to the white that dazzled round it, gave somewhat the idea of a pink slash in the glossiest white satin. Her gallant, who was a gentleman about thirty, somewhat inclin'd to a fatness that was in no sort displeasing, improving the hint thus tendered him of this mode of enjoyment, after settling her well in this posture, and encouraging her with kisses and caresses to stand him through, drew out his affair ready erected, and whose extreme length, rather disproportion'd to its breadth, was the more surprising, as that excess is not often the case with those of his corpulent habit; making then the right and direct application, he drove it up to the guard, whilst the round bulge of those Turkish beauties of her's tallying with the hollow made with the bent of his belly and thighs, as they curved inwards, brought all those parts, surely not undelightfully, into warm touch, and close conjunction; his hands he kept passing round her body, and employed in toying with her enchanting breasts. As soon too as she felt him at home as he could reach, she lifted her head a little from the pillow, and turning her neck, without much straining, but her cheeks glowing with the deepest scarlet, and a smile of the tenderest satisfaction, met the kiss he press'd forward to give her as they were thus close joined together: when leaving him to pursue his delights, she hid again her face and blushes with her hands and pillow, and thus stood passively and as favourably too as she could, whilst he kept laying at her with repeated thrusts and making the meeting flesh on both sides resound again with the violence of them; then ever as he backen'd from her, we could see between them part of his long whitestaff foamingly in motion, till, as he went on again and closed with her, the interposing hillocks took it out of sight. Sometimes he took his hands from the semi-globes of her bosoms, and transferred the pressure of them to those larger ones, the present subjects of his soft blockade, which he squeez'd, grasp'd and play'd with, till at length a pursuit of driving, so hotly urged, brought on the height of the fit, with such overpowering pleasure, that his fair partner became, now necessary to support him, panting, fainting and dying as he discharged; which she no sooner felt the killing sweetness of, than unable to keep her legs, and yielding to the mighty intoxication, she reeled, and falling forward on the couch, made it a necessity for him, if he would preserve the warm pleasurehold, to fall upon her, where they perfected, in a continued conjunction of body and ecstatic flow, their scheme of joys for that time.

As soon as he had disengag'd, the charming Emily got up, and we crowded round her with congratulations and other officious little services; for it is to be noted, that though all modesty and reserve were banished from the transaction of these pleasures, good manners and politeness were inviolably observ'd: here was no gross ribaldry, no offensive or rude behaviour, or ungenerous reproaches to the girls for their compliance with the humours and desires of the men. On the contrary, nothing was wanting to soothe, encourage, and soften the sense of their condition to them. Men know not in general how much they destroy of their own pleasure, when they break through the respect and tenderness due to our sex, and even to those of it who live only by pleasing them. And this was a maxim perfectly well understood by

THE SCARLET LIBRARY

these polite voluptuaries, these profound adepts in the great art and science of pleasure, who never shew'd these votaries of theirs a more tender respect than at the time of those exercises of their complaisance, when they unlock'd their treasures of concealed beauty, and shewed out in the pride of their native charms, ever-more touching surely than when they paraded it in the artificial ones of dress and ornament.

The frolick was now come round to me, and it being my turn of subscription to the will and pleasure of my particular elect, as well as to that of the company, he came to me, and saluting me very tenderly, with a flattering eagerness, put me in mind of the compliances my presence there authoris'd the hopes of, and at the same time repeated to me that if all this force of example had not surmounted any repugnance I might have to concur with the humours and desires of the company, that though the play was bespoke for my benefit, and great as his own private disappointment might be, he would suffer any thing, sooner than be the instrument of imposing a disagreeable task on me.

To this I answered, without the least hesitation or mincing grimace, that had I not even contracted a kind of engagement to be at his disposal without the least reserve, the example of such agreeable companions would alone determine me and that I was in no pain about any thing but my appearing to so great a disadvantage after such superior beauties. And take notice that I thought as I spoke. The frankness of the answer pleas'd them all; my particular was complimented on his acquisition, and, by way of indirect flattery to me, openly envied.

Mrs. Cole, by the way, could not have given me a greater mark of her regard than in managing for me the choice of this young gentleman for my master of the ceremonies: for, independent of his noble birth and the great fortune he was heir to, his person was even uncommonly pleasing, well shaped and tall; his face mark'd with the small-pox, but no more than what added a grace of more manliness to features rather turned to softness and delicacy, was marvellously enliven'd by eyes which were of the clearest sparkling black; in short, he was one whom any woman would, in the familiar style, readily call a very pretty fellow.

I was now handed by him to the cock-pit of our match, where, as I was dressed in nothing but a white morning gown, he vouchsafed to play the male-Abigail on this occasion, and spared me the confusion that would have attended the forwardness of undressing myself: my gown then was loosen'd in a trice, and I divested of it; my stay next offered an obstacle which readily gave way, Louisa very readily furnishing a pair of scissors to cut the lace; off went that shell and dropping my upper-coat, I was reduced to my under one and my shift, the open bosom of which gave the hands and eyes all the liberty they could wish. Here I imagin'd the stripping was to stop, but I reckoned short: my spark, at the desire of the rest, tenderly begged that I would not suffer the small remains of a covering to rob them of a full view of my whole person; and for me, who was too flexibly obsequious to dispute any point with them, and who considered the little more that remain'd as very immaterial, I readily assented to whatever he pleased. In an instant, then, my under-petticoat was untied and at my feet, and my shift drawn over my head, so that my cap, slightly fasten'd, came off with it, and brought all my hair down (of which, be it again remembered without vanity, that I had a very fine head) in loose disorderly ringlets, over my neck and shoulders, to the not unfavourable set-off of my skin.

I now stood before my judges in all the truth of nature, to whom I could not appear a very disagreeable figure, if you please to recollect what I have before said of my person, which time, that at certain periods of life robs us every instant of our charms, had, at that of mine, then greatly improved into full and open bloom, for I wanted some months of eighteen. My breasts, which in the state of nudity are ever capital points, now in no more than in graceful plenitude, maintained a firmness and steady independence of any stay or support that dared and invited the test of the touch. Then I was as tall, as slim-shaped as could be consistent with all that juicy plumpness of flesh, ever the most grateful to the senses of sight and touch, which I owed to the health and youth of my constitution. I had not, however, so thoroughly renounc'd all innate shame as not to suffer great confusion at the state I saw myself in; but the whole troop round me, men and women, relieved me with every mark of applause and satisfaction, every flattering attention to raise and inspire me with even sentiments of pride on the figure I made, which, my friend gallantly protested, infinitely outshone all other birthday finery whatever; so that had I leave to set down, for sincere, all the compliments these connoisseurs overwhelmed me with upon this occasion, I might flatter myself with having pass'd my examination with the approbation of the learned.

My friend however, who for this time had alone the disposal of me, humoured their curiosity, and perhaps his own, so far that he placed me in all the variety of postures and lights imaginable, pointing out every beauty under every aspect of it, not without such parentheses of kisses, such inflammatory liberties of his roving hands, as made all shame fly before them, and a blushing glow give place to a warmer one of desire, which led me even to find some relish in the present scene.

But in this general survey, you may be sure, the most material spot of me was not excus'd the strictest visitation; nor was it but agreed, that I had not the least reason to be diffident of passing even for a maid, on occasion: so inconsiderable a flaw had my preceding adventures created there, and so soon had the blemish of an over-stretch been repaired and worn out at my age, and in my naturally small make in that part.

Now, whether my partner had exhausted all the modes of regaling the touch or sight, or whether he was now ungovernably wound up to strike, I know not; but briskly throwing off his clothes, the prodigious heat bred by a close room, a great fire, numerous candles, and even the inflammatory warmth of these scenes, induced him to lay aside his shirt too, when his breeches, before loosen'd, now gave up their contents to view, and shew'd in front the enemy I had to engage with, stiffly bearing up the port of its head unhooded, and glowing red. Then I plainly saw what I had to trust to: it was one of those just true-siz'd instruments, of which the masters have a better command than the more unwieldy, inordinate siz'd ones are generally under. Straining me then close to his bosom, as he stood up fore-right against me and applying to the obvious niche its peculiar idol, he aimed at inserting it, which, as I forwardly favoured, he effected at once by canting up my thighs over his naked hips, and made me receive every inch, and close home; so that stuck upon the pleasure-pivot, and clinging round his neck, in which and in his hair I hid my face, burningly flushing with my present feelings as much as with shame, my bosom glew'd to his; he carried me once round the couch, on which he then, without quitting the middle-fastness, or dischannelling, laid me down, and began the pleasure-grist. But so provokingly predisposed and primed as we were, by all the moving sights of the night, our imagination was too much heated not to melt us of the soonest: and accordingly, I no sooner felt the warm spray darted up my inwards from him, but I was punctually on flow, to share the momentary ecstasy; but I had yet greater reason to boast of our harmony: for finding that all the flames of desire were not yet quench'd within me, but that rather, like wetted coals, I glowed the fiercer for this sprinkling, my hot-mettled spark, sympathizing with me, and loaded for a double fire, recontinu'd the sweet battery with undying vigour; greatly pleas'd at which I gratefully endeavoured to accommodate all my motions to his best advantage and delight; kisses, squeezes, tender murmurs, all came into play, till our joys, growing more turbulent and riotous, threw us into a fond disorder, and as they raged to a point, bore us far from ourselves into an ocean of boundless pleasures, into which we both plunged together in a transport of taste. Now all the impressions of burning desire, from the lively scenes I had been spectatress of, ripened by the heat of this exercise, and collecting to a head, throbb'd and agitated me with insupportable irritations: I did not now enjoy a calm of reason enough to perceive, but I ecstatically, indeed, felt the power of such rare and exquisite provocatives, as the examples of the night had proved towards thus exalting our pleasures: which, with great joy, I sensibly found my gallant shared in, by his nervous and home expressions of it: his eyes flashing eloquent flames, his action infuriated with the stings of it, all conspiring to rise my delight by assuring me of his. Lifted then to the utmost pitch of joy that human life can bear, undestroyed by excess, I touch'd that sweetly critical point, whence scarce prevented by the injection from my partner, I dissolved, and breaking out into a deep drawn sigh, sent my whole sensitive soul down to that passage where escape was denied it, by its being so deliciously plugged and chok'd up. Thus we lay a few blissful instants, overpowered, still, and languid; till, as the sense of pleasure stagnated, we recover'd from our trance, and he slipt out of me, not however before he had protested his extreme satisfaction by the tenderest kiss and embrace, as well as by the most cordial expressions.

The company, who had stood round us in a profound silence, when all was over, help'd me to hurry on my cloaths in an instant, and complimented me on the sincere homage they could not escape observing had been done (as they termed it) to the sovereignty of my charms, in my receiving a double payment of tribute at one juncture. But my partner, now dress'd again, signalis'd, above all, a fondness unbated by the circumstance of recent enjoyment; the girls too kiss'd and embraced me, assuring me that for that time, or indeed any other, unless I pleased, I was to go thro' no farther publick trials, and that I was now consummatedly initiated, and one of them.

As it was an inviolable law for every gallant to keep to his partner, for the night especially, and even till he relinquish'd possession over to the community, in order to preserve a pleasing property and to avoid the disgusts and indelicacy of another arrangement, the company, after a short refection of biscuits and wine, tea and chocolate, served in at now about one in the morning, broke up, and went off in pairs. Mrs. Cole had prepared my spark and me an occasional field-bed, to which we retir'd, and there ended the night in one continued strain of pleasure, sprightly and uncloy'd enough for us not to have formed one wish for its ever knowing an end. In the morning, after a restorative breakfast in bed, he got up, and with very tender assurances of a particular regard for me, left me to the composure and refreshment of a sweet slumber; waking out of which, and getting up to dress before Mrs. Cole should come in, I found in one of my pockets a purse of guineas, which he had slipt there; and just as I was musing on a liberality I had certainly not expected, Mrs. Cole came in, to whom I immediately communicated the present, and naturally offered her whatever share she pleas'd: but assuring me that the gentleman had very nobly rewarded her, she would on no terms, no entreaties, no shape I could put it in, receive any part of it. Her denial, she observed, was not affectation of grimace, and proceeded to read me such admirable lessons on the economy of my person and my purse as I became amply paid for my general attention and conformity to in the course of my acquaintance with the town. After which, changing the discourse, she fell on the pleasures of the preceding night, where I learn'd, without much surprise, as I began to enter on her character, that she had seen every thing that had passed, from a convenient place managed solely for that purpose, and of which she readily made me the confidante.

She had scarce finish'd this, when the little troop of love, the girls my companions, broke in and renewed their compliments and caresses. I observed with pleasure that the fatigues and exercises of the night had not usurped in the least on the life of their complexion, or the freshness of their bloom: this I found, by their confession, was owing to the management and advice of our rare directress. They went down then to figure it, as usual, in the shop, whilst I repair'd to my lodgings, where I employed myself till I returned to dinner at Mrs. Cole's.

Here I staid in constant amusement, with one or other of these charming girls, till about five in the evening; when seiz'd with a sudden drowsy fit, I was prevailed on to go up and doze it off on Harriet's bed, who left me on it to my repose. There then I lay down in my cloaths and fell fast asleep, and had now enjoyed, by guess, about an hour's rest, when I was pleasingly disturbed by my new and favourite gallant, who, enquiring for me, was readily directed where to find me. Coming then into my chamber, and seeing me lie alone, with my face turn'd from the light towards the inside of the bed, he, without more ado, just slipped off his breeches, for the greater ease and enjoyment of the naked touch; and softly turning up my petticoat and shift behind, opened the prospect of the back avenue to the genial seat of pleasure; where, as I lay at my side length, inclining rather face downward, I appeared full fair, and liable to be entered. Laying himself then gently down by me, he invested me behind, and giving me to feel the warmth of his body as he applied his thighs and belly close to me, and the endeavours of that machine, whose touch has something so exquisitely singular in it, to make its way good into me. I wak'd pretty much startled at first, but seeing who it was, disposed myself to turn to him, when he gave me a kiss, and desiring me to keep my posture, just lifted up my upper thigh, and ascertaining the right opening, soon drove it up to the farthest: satisfied with which, and solacing himself with lying so close in those parts, he suspended motion, and thus steeped in pleasure, kept me lying on my side, into him, spoon-fashion, as he term'd it, from the snug indent of the back part of my thighs, and all upwards, into the space of the bending between his thighs and belly; till, after some time, that restless and turbulent inmate, impatient by nature of longer quiet, urg'd him to action, which now prosecuting with all the usual train of toying, kissing, and the like, ended at length in the liquid proof on both sides, that we had not exhausted, or at least were quickly recruited of last night's draughts of pleasure in us.

With this noble and agreeable youth liv'd I in perfect joy and constancy. He was full bent on keeping me to himself, for the honey-month at least; but his stay in London was not even so long, his father, who had a post in Ireland, taking him abruptly with him on his repairing thither. Yet even then I was near keeping hold of his affection and person, as he had propos'd, and I had consented to follow him in order to go to Ireland after him, as soon as he could be settled there; but meeting with an agreeable and advantageous match in that kingdom, he chose the wiser part, and forebore sending for me, but at the same time took care that I should receive a very magnificent present, which did not however compensate for all my deep regret on my loss of him.

This event also created a chasm in our little society, which Mrs. Cole, on the foot of her usual caution, was in no haste to fill up; but then it redoubled her attention to procure me, in the advantages of a traffic for a counterfeit maidenhead, some consolation for the sort of widowhood I had been left in; and this was a scheme she had never lost prospect of, and only waited for a proper person to bring it to bear with.

But I was, it seems, fated to be my own caterer in this, as I had been in my first trial of the market.

I had now pass'd near a month in the enjoyment of all the pleasures of familiarity and society with my companions, whose particular favourites (the baronet excepted, who soon after took Harriet home) had all, on the terms of community establish'd in the house, solicited the gratification of their taste for variety in my embraces; but I had with the utmost art and address, on various pretexts, eluded their pursuit, without giving them cause to complain; and this reserve I used neither out of dislike of them, or disgust of the thing, but my true reason was my attachment to my own, and my tenderness of invading the choice of my companions, who outwardly exempt, as they seem'd, from jealousy, could not but in secret like me the better for the regard I had for, without making a merit of it to them. Thus easy, and beloved by the whole family, did I go on; when one day, that, about five in the afternoon, I stepped over to a fruiterer's shop in Covent Garden, to pick some table fruit for myself and the young women, I met with the following adventure.

Whilst I was chaffering for the fruit I wanted, I observ'd myself follow'd by a young gentleman, whose rich dress first attracted my notice; for the rest, he had nothing remarkable in his person, except that he was pale, thin-made, and ventur'd himself upon legs rather of the slenderest. Easy was it to perceive, without seeming to perceive it, that it was me he wanted to be at; and keeping his eyes fixed on me, till he came to the same basket that I stood at, and cheapening, or rather giving the first price ask'd for the fruit, began his approaches. Now most certainly I was not at all out of figure to pass for a modest girl. I had neither the feathers nor *fumet* of a taudry townmiss: a straw hat, a white gown, clean linen, and above all, a certain natural and easy air of modesty (which the appearances of never forsook me, even on those occasions that I most broke in upon it, in practice) were all signs that gave him no opening to conjecture my condition. He spoke to me; and this address from a stranger throwing a blush into my cheeks that still set him wider off the truth, I answered him with an awkwardness and confusion the more apt to impose, as there was really a mixture of the genuine in them. But when proceeding, on the foot of having broken the ice, to join discourse, he went into other leading questions, I put so much innocence, simplicity, and even childishness into my answers that on no better foundation, liking my person as he did, I will answer for it, he would have been sworn for my modesty. There is, in short, in the men, when once they are caught, by the eye especially, a fund of cullibility that their lordly wisdom little dreams of, and in virtue of which the most sagacious of them are seen so often our dupes. Amongst other queries he put to me, one was whether I was married.

I replied that I was too young to think of that this many a year. To that of my age, I answered, and sunk a year upon him, passing myself for not seventeen. As to my way of life, I told him I had serv'd an apprenticeship to a milliner in Preston, and was come to town after a relation, that I had found, on my arrival, was dead, and now liv'd journey-woman to a milliner in town. That last article, indeed, was not much of the side of what I pretended to pass for; but it did pass, under favour of the growing passion I had inspir'd him with. After he had next got out of me, very dextrously as he thought, what I had no sort of design to make reserve of, my own, my mistress's name, and place of abode, he loaded me with fruit, all the rarest and dearest he could pick out, and sent me home, pondering on what might be the consequence of this adventure.

As soon then as I came to Mrs. Cole's, I related to her all that passed, on which she very judiciously concluded that if he did not come after me there was no harm done, and that, if he did, as her presage suggested to her he would, his character and his views should be well sifted, so as to know whether the game was worth the springs; that in the mean time nothing was easier than my part in it, since no more rested on me than to follow her cue and promptership throughout, to the last act.

The next morning, after an evening spent on his side, as we afterwards learnt, in perquisitions into Mrs. Cole's character in the neighbourhood (than which nothing could be more favourable to her design upon him), my gentleman came in his chariot to the shop, where Mrs. Cole alone had an inkling of his errand. Asking then for her, he easily made a beginning of acquaintance by be-speaking some millinery ware: when, as I sat without lifting up my eyes, and pursuing the hem of a ruffle with the utmost composure and simplicity of industry, Mrs. Cole took notice that the first impressions I made on him ran no risk of being destroyed by those of Louisa and Emily, who were then sitting at work by me. After vainly endeavouring to catch my eyes in re-encounter with his (as I held my head down, affecting a kind of consciousness of guilt for having, by speaking to him, given him encouragement and means of following me), and after giving Mrs. Cole direction when to bring the things home herself, and the time he should expect them, he went out, taking with him some goods that he paid for liberally, for the better grace of his introduction.

PART VIII

The girls all this time did not in the least smoke the mystery of this new customer; but Mrs. Cole, as soon as we were conveniently alone, insur'd me, in virtue of her long experience in these matters, that for this bout my charms had not miss'd fire; for that by his eagerness, his manner and looks, she was sure he had it: the only point now in doubt was his character and circumstances, which her knowledge of the town would soon gain her sufficient acquaintance with, to take her measures upon.

And effectively, in a few hours, her intelligence serv'd her so well that she learn'd that this conquest of mine was no other than Mr. Norbert, a gentleman originally of great fortune, which, with a constitution naturally not the best, he had vastly impaired by his over-violent pursuit of the vices of the town; in the course of which, having worn out and stal'd all the more common modes of debauchery, he had fallen into a taste of maiden-hunting; in which chase he had ruin'd a number of girls, sparing no expense to compass his ends, and generally using them well till tired, or cool'd by enjoyment, or springing a new face, he could with more ease disembarrass himself of the old ones, and resign them to their fate, as his sphere of achievements of that sort lay only amongst such as he could proceed with by way of bargain and sale.

Concluding from these premises, Mrs. Cole observ'd that a character of this sort was ever a lawful prize; that the sin would be, not to make the best of our market of him; and that she thought such a girl as I only too good for him at any rate, and on any terms.

She went then, at the hour appointed, to his lodgings in one of our inns of court, which were furnished in a taste of grandeur that had a special eye to all the conveniences of luxury and pleasure. Here she found him in ready waiting; and after finishing her pretence of business, and a long circuit of discussions concerning her trade, which she said was very bad, the qualities of her servants, 'prentices, journey-women, the discourse naturally landed at length on me, when Mrs. Cole, acting admirably the good old prating gossip, who lets every thing escape her when her tongue is set in motion, cooked him up a story so plausible of me, throwing in every now and then such strokes of art, with all the simplest air of nature, in praise of my person and temper, as finished him finely for her purpose, whilst nothing could be better counterfeited than her innocence of his. But when now fired and on edge, he proceeded to drop hints of his design and views upon me, after he had with much confusion and pains brought her to the point (she kept as long aloof from as she thought proper) of understanding him, without now affecting to pass for a dragoness of virtue, by flying out into those violent and ever suspicious passions, she stuck with the better grace and effect to the character of a plain, good sort of a woman, that knew no harm, and that getting her bread in an honest way, was made of stuff easy and flexible enough to be wrought upon to his ends, by his superior skill and address; but, however, she managed so artfully that three or four meetings took place before he could obtain the least favourable hope of her assistance; without which, he had, by a number of fruitless messages, letters, and other direct trials of my disposition, convinced himself there was no coming at me, all which too rais'd at once my character and price with him.

Regardful, however, of not carrying these difficulties to such a length as might afford time for starting discoveries, or incidents, unfavourable to her plan, she at last pretended to be won over by mere dint of entreaties, promises, and, above all, by the dazzling sum she took care to wind him up to the specification of, when it was now even a piece of art to feign, at once, a yielding to the allurements of a great interest, as a pretext for her yielding at all, and the manner of it such as might persuade him she had never dipp'd her virtuous fingers in an affair of that sort.

Thus she led him through all the gradations of difficulty, and obstacles, necessary to enhance the value of the prize he aim'd at; and in conclusion, he was so struck with the little beauty I was mistress of, and so eagerly bent on gaining his ends of me, that he left her even no room to boast of her management in bringing him up to her mark, he drove so plum of himself into every thing tending to make him swallow the bait. Not but, in other respects, Mr. Norbert was not clear sighted enough, or that he did not perfectly know the town, and even by experience, the very branch of imposition now in practice upon him: but we had his passion our friend so much, he was so blinded and hurried on by it, that he would have thought any undeception a very ill office done to his pleasure. Thus concurring, even precipitately, to the point she wanted him at, Mrs. Cole brought him at last to hug himself on the cheap bargain he consider'd the purchase of my imaginary jewel was to him, at no more than three hundred guineas to myself, and a hundred to the brokeress: being a slender recompense for all her pains, and all the scruples of conscience she had now sacrificed to him for this the first time of her life; which sums were to be paid down on the nail, upon livery of my person, exclusive of some no inconsiderable presents that had been made in the course of the negotiation: during which I had occasionally, but sparingly been introduc'd into his company, at proper times and hours; in which it is incredible how little it seem'd necessary to strain my natural disposition to modesty higher, in order to pass it upon him for that of a very maid: all my looks and gestures ever breathing nothing but that innocence which the men so ardently require in us, for no other end than to feast themselves with the pleasures of destroying it, and which they are so grievously, with all their skill, subject to mistakes in.

When the articles of the treaty had been fully agreed on, the stipulated payments duly secur'd, and nothing now remained but the execution of the main point, which center'd in the surrender of my person up to his free disposal and use, Mrs. Cole managed her objections, especially to his lodgings, and insinuations so nicely, that it became his own mere notion and urgent request that this copy of a wedding should be finish'd at her house: At first, indeed, she did not care, said she, to have such doings in it – she would not for a thousand pounds have any of the servants or 'prentices know it – her precious good name would be gone forever – with the like excuses. However, on superior objections to all other expedients, whilst she took care to start none but those which were most liable to them, it came round at last to the necessity of her obliging him in that conveniency, and of doing a little more where she had already done so much.

The night then was fix'd, with all possible respect to the eagerness of his impatience, and in the mean time Mrs. Cole had omitted no instructions, nor even neglected any preparation, that might enable me to come off with honour, in regard to the appearance of my virginity, except that, favour'd as I was by nature with all the narrowness of stricture in that part requisite to conduct my designs, I had no occasion to borrow those auxiliaries of art that create a momentary one, easily discover'd by the test of a warm bath; and as to the usual sanguinary symptoms of defloration, which, if not always, are generally attendants on it, Mrs. Cole had made me the mistress of an invention of her own which could hardly miss its effect, and of which more in its place.

Everything then being disposed and fix'd for Mr. Norbert's reception, he was, at the hour of eleven at night, with all the mysteries of silence and secrecy, let in by Mrs. Cole herself, and introduced into her bed-chamber, where, in an old-fashioned bed of her's, I lay, fully undressed, and panting, if not with the fears of a real maid, at least with those perhaps greater of a dissembled one which gave me an air of confusion and bashfulness that maiden-modesty had all the honour of, and was indeed scarce distinguishable from it, even by less partial eyes than those of my lover: so let me call him, for I ever thought the term "cully" too cruel a reproach to the men for their abused weakness for us.

As soon as Mrs. Cole, after the old gossipery, on these occasions, us'd to young women abandoned for the first time to the will of man, had left us alone in her room, which, bythe-bye, was well lighted up, at his previous desire, that seemed to bode a stricter examination that he afterwards made, Mr. Norbert, still dressed, sprung towards the bed, where I got my head under the cloaths, and defended them a good while before he could even get at my lips, to kiss them: so true it is, that a false virtue, on this occasion, even makes a greater rout and resistance than a true one. From thence he descended to my breasts, the feel I disputed tooth and nail with him till, tired with my resistance, and thinking probably to give a better account of me, when got into bed to me, he hurry'd his cloaths off in an instant, and came into bed.

Mean while, by the glimpse I stole of him, I could easily discover a person far from promising any such doughty performances as the storming of maidenheads generally requires, and whose flimsy consumptive texture gave him more the air of an invalid that was pressed, than of a volunteer, on such hot service.

At scarce thirty, he had already reduced his strength of appetite down to a wretched dependence on forc'd provocatives, very little seconded by the natural power of a body jaded and racked off to the lees by constant repeated over-draughts of pleasure, which had done the work of sixty winters on his springs of life: leaving him at the same time all the fire and heat of youth in his imagination, which served at once to torment and spur him down the precipice.

As soon as he was in bed, he threw off the bed-cloaths, which I suffered him to force from my hold, and I now lay as expos'd as he could wish, not only to his attacks, but his visitation of the sheets; where in the various agitations of the body, through my endeavours to defend myself, he could easily assure himself there was no preparation: though, to do him justice, he seem'd a less strict examinant than I had apprehended from so experienc'd a practitioner. My shift then he fairly tore open, finding I made too much use of it to barricade my breasts, as well as the more important avenue: yet in every thing else he proceeded with all the marks of tenderness and regard to me, whilst the art of my play was to shew none for him. I acted then all the niceties, apprehensions, and terrors supposable for a girl perfectly innocent to feel at so great a novelty as a naked man in bed with her for the first time. He scarce even obtained a kiss but what he ravished; I put his hand away twenty times from my breasts, where he had satisfied himself of their hardness and consistence, with passing for hitherto unhandled goods. But when grown impatient for the main point, he now threw himself upon me, and first trying to examine me with his finger, sought to make himself further way, I complained of his usage bitterly: I thought he would not have serv'd a body so – I was ruin'd – I did not know what I had done – I would get up, so I would – and at the same time kept my thighs so fast locked, that it was not for strength like his to force them open, or do any good. Finding thus my advantages, and that I had both my own and his motions at command, the deceiving him came so easy that it was perfectly playing upon velvet. In the mean time his machine, which was one of those sizes that slip in and out without being minded, kept pretty stiffly bearing against that part, which the shutting my thighs barr'd access to; but finding, at length, he could do no good by mere dint of bodily strength, he resorted to entreaties and arguments: to which I only answer'd with a tone of shame and timidity, that I was afraid he would kill me – Lord! – , I would not be served so – I was never so used in all my born days – I wondered he was not ashamed of himself, so I did – , with such silly infantile moods of repulse and complaint as I judged best adapted to the express the character of innocence and affright. Pretending, however, to yield at length to the vehemence of his insistence, in action and words, I sparingly disclosed my thighs, so that he could just touch the cloven inlet with the tip of his instrument: but as he fatigued and toil'd to get it in, a twist of my body, so as to receive it obliquely, not only thwarted his admission, but giving a scream, as if he had pierced me to the heart, I shook him off me with such violence that he could not with all his might to it, keep the saddle: vex'd indeed at this he seemed, but not in the style of any displeasure with me for my skittishness; on the contrary, I dare swear he held me the dearer, and hugged himself for the difficulties that even hurt his instant pleasure. Fired, however, now beyond all bearance of delay, he remounts and begg'd of me to have patience, stroking and soothing me to it by all the tenderest endearments and protestations of what he would moreover do for me; at which, feigning to be something softened, and abating of the anger that I had shewn at his hurting me so prodigiously, I suffered him to lay my thighs aside, and make way for a new trial; but I watched the directions and management of his point so well, that no sooner was the orifice in the least open to it, but I gave such a timely jerk as seemed to proceed not from the evasion of his entry, but from the pain his efforts at it put me to: a circumstance too that I did not fail to accompany with proper gestures, sighs and cries of complaint, of which that he had hurt me – he kill'd me – I should die – , were the most frequent interjections. But now, after repeated attempts, in which he had not made the least impression towards gaining his point, at least for that time, the pleasure rose so fast upon him that he could not check or delay it, and in the vigour and fury which the approaches of the height of it inspir'd him, he made one fierce thrust, that had almost put me by my guard, and lodged it so far that I could feel the warm inspersion just within the exterior orifice, which I had the cruelty not to let him finish there, but threw him out again, not without a most piercing loud exclamation, as if the pain had put me beyond all regard of being overheard. It was easy then to observe that he was more satisfy'd, more highly pleased with the supposed motives of his baulk of consummation, than he would have been at the full attainment of it. It was on this foot that I solved to myself all the falsity I employed to procure him that blissful pleasure in it, which most certainly he would not have tasted in the truth of things. Eas'd however, and relieved by one discharge, he now apply'd himself to sooth, encourage and to put me into humour and patience to bear his next attempt, which he began to prepare and gather force for, from all the incentives of the touch and sight which he could think of, by examining every individual part of my whole body, which he declared his satisfaction with in raptures of applauses, kisses universally imprinted, and sparing no part of me, in all the eagerest wantonness of feeling, seeing, and toying. His vigour however did not return so soon, and I felt him more than once pushing at the door, but so little in a condition to break in, that I question whether he had the power to enter, had I held it ever so open; but this he then thought me too little acquainted with the nature of things to have any regret or confusion about, and he kept fatiguing himself and me for a long time, before he was in any state to resume his attacks with any prospect of success; and then I breath'd him so warmly, and kept him so at bay, that before he had made any sensible progress in point of penetration, he was deliciously sweated, and weary'd out indeed: so that it was deep in the morning before he achieved his second let-go, about half way of entrance, I all the while crying and complaining of his prodigious vigour, and the immensity of what I appear'd to suffer splitting up with. Tired, however, at length, with such athletic drudgery, my champion began now to give out, and to gladly embrace the refreshment of some rest. Kissing me then with much affection, and recommending me to my repose, he presently fell fast asleep: which, as soon as I had well satisfy'd myself of, I with much composure of body, so as not to wake him by any motion, with much ease and safety too, played of Mrs. Cole's advice for perfecting the signs of my virginity.

In each of the head bed-posts, just above where the bedsteads are inserted into them, there was a small drawer, so artfully adapted to the mouldings of the timber-work, that it might have escap'd even the most curious search: which drawers were easily open'd or shut by the touch of a spring, and were fitted each with a shallow glass tumbler, full of a prepared fluid blood, in which lay soak'd, for ready use, a sponge that required no more than gently reaching the hand to it, taking it out and properly squeezing between the thighs, when it yielded a great deal more of the red liquid than would save a girl's honour; after which, replacing it, and touching the spring, all possibility of discovery, or even of suspicion, was taken away; and all this was not the work of the fourth part of a minute, and on which ever side one lay, the thing was equally easy and practicable, by the double care taken to have each bed-post provided alike. True it is, that had he waked and caught me in the act, it would at least have covered me with shame and confusion; but then, that he did not, was, with the precautions I took, a risk of a thousand to one in my favour.

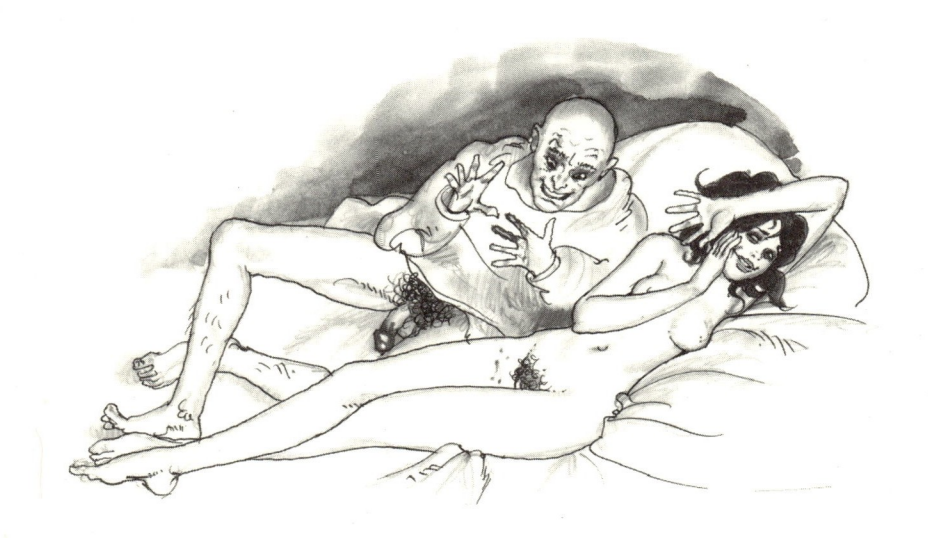

At ease now, and out of all fear of any doubt or suspicion

on his side, I address'd myself in good earnest to my repose, but could obtain none; and in about half an hour's time my gentleman waked again, and turning towards me, I feigned a sound sleep, which he did not long respect; but girding himself again to renew the onset, he began to kiss and caress me, when now making as if I just wak'd, I complained of the disturbance, and of the cruel pain that this little rest had stole my senses from. Eager, however, for the pleasure, as well of consummating an entire triumph over my virginity, he said everything that could overcome my resistance, and bribe my patience to the end, which not I was ready to listen to, from being secure of the bloody proofs I had prepared of his victorious violence, though I still thought it good policy not to let him in yet a while. I answered then only to his importunities in sighs and moans that I was so hurt, I could not bear it – I was sure he had done me a mischief; that he had – he was such a sad man! At this, turning down the cloaths and viewing the field of battle by the glimmer of a dying taper, he saw plainly my thighs, shift, and sheets, all stained with what he readily took for a virgin effusion, proceeding from his last halfpenetration: convinc'd, and transported at which, nothing could equal his joy and exultation. The illusion was complete, no other conception entered his head but that of his having been at work upon an unopen'd mine; which idea, upon so strong an evidence, redoubled at once his tenderness for me, and his ardour for breaking it wholly up. Kissing me then with the utmost rapture, he comforted me, and begg'd my pardon for the pain he had put me to: observing withal, that it was only a thing in course: but the worst was certainly past, and that with a little courage and constancy, I should get it once well over, and never after experience any thing but the greatest pleasure. By little and little I suffer'd myself to be prevailed on, and giving, as it were, up the point to him, I made my thighs, insensibly spreading them, yield him liberty of access, which improving, he got a little within me, when by a well managed reception I work'd the female screw so nicely, that I kept him from the easy mid-channel direction, and by dextrous wreathing and contortions, creating an artificial difficulty of entrance, made him win it inch by inch, with the most laborious struggles, I all the while sorely complaining: till at length, with might and main, winding his way in, he got it completely home, and giving my virginity, as he thought, the *coup de grace*, furnished me with the cue of setting up a terrible outcry, whilst he, triumphant and like a cock clapping his wings over his down-trod mistress, pursu'd his pleasure: which presently rose, in virtue of this idea of a complete victory, to a pitch that made me soon sensible of his melting period; whilst I now lay acting the deep wounded, breathless, frighten'd, undone, no longer maid.

You would ask me, perhaps, whether all this time I enjoy'd any perception of pleasure? I assure you, little or none, till just towards the latter end, a faintish sense of it came on mechanically, from so long a struggle and frequent fret in that ever sensible part; but, in the first place, I had no taste for the person I was suffering the embraces of, on a pure mercenary account; and then, I was not entirely delighted with myself for the jade's part I was playing, whatever excuses I might have to plead for my being brought into it; but then this insensibility kept me so much the mistress of my mind and motions, that I could the better manage so close a counterfeit, through the whole scene of deception.

Recover'd at length to a more shew of life, by his tender condolences, kisses and embraces, I upbraided him, and reproach'd him with my ruin, in such natural terms as added to his satisfaction with himself for having accomplish'd it; and guessing, by certain observations of mine, that it would be rather favourable to him, to spare him, when he some time after, feebly enough, came on again to the assault, I resolutely withstood any further endeavours, on a pretext that flattered his prowess, of my being so violently hurt and sore that I could not possibly endure a fresh trial. He then graciously granted me a respite, and the next morning soon after advancing, I got rid of further importunity, till Mrs. Cole, being rang for by him, came in and was made acquainted, in terms of the utmost joy and rapture, with his triumphant certainty of my virtue, and the finishing stroke he had given it in the course of the night: of which, he added, she would see proof enough in bloody characters on the sheets.

You may guess how a woman of her turn of address and experience humour'd the jest, and played him off with mixed exclamations of shame, anger, compassion for me, and of her being pleased that all was so well over: in which last, I believe, she was certainly sincere. And now, as the objection which she had represented as an invincible one, to my lying the first night at his lodgings (which were studiously calculated for freedom of intrigues), on the account of my maiden fears and terrors at the thoughts of going to a gentleman's chambers, and being alone with him in bed, was surmounted, she pretended to persuade me, in favour to him, that I should go there to him whenever he pleas'd, and still keep up all the necessary appearances of working with her, that I might not lose, with my character, the prospect of getting a good husband, and at the same time her house would be kept the safer from scandal. All this seem'd so reasonable, so considerate to Mr. Norbert, that he never once perceived that she did not want him to resort to her house, lest he might in time discover certain inconsistencies with the character she had set out with to him: besides that, this plan greatly flattered his own ease, and views of liberty. Leaving me then to my much wanted rest, he got up, and Mrs. Cole, after settling with him all points relating to the composure of cooler thoughts. However, he seiz'd me as a prize, and without farther ceremony threw his arms round my neck and kiss'd me boisterously and sweetly. I looked at him with a beginning of anger and indignation at his rudeness, that softened away into other sentiments as I viewed him: for he was tall, manly carriaged, handsome of body and face, so that I ended my stare with asking him, in a tone turn'd to tenderness, what he meant; at which, with the same frankness and vivacity as he had begun with me, he proposed treating me with a glass of wine. Now, certain it is, that had I been in a calmer state of blood than I was, had I not been under the dominion of unappeas'd irritations and desires, I should have refused him without hesitation; but I do not know how it was, my pressing calls, his figure, the occasion, and if you will, the powerful combination of all these, with a start of curiosity to see the end of an adventure, so novel too as being treated like a common street-plyer, made me give a silent consent; in short, it was not my head that I now obeyed, I suffered myself to be towed along as it were by this man-of-war, who took me under his arm as familiarly as if he had known me all his life-time, and led me into the next convenient tavern, where we were shewn into a little room on one side of the passage. Here, scarce allowing himself patience till the waiter brought in the wine call'd for, he fell directly on board me: when, untucking my handkerchief, and giving me a snatching buss, he laid my breasts bare at once, which he handled with that keenness of lust that abridges a ceremonial ever more tiresome than pleasing on such pressing occasions; and now, hurrying towards the main point, we found no conveniency to our purpose, two or three disabled chairs and a rickety table composing the whole furniture of the room. Without more ado, he plants me with my back standing against the wall, and my petticoats up; and coming out with a splitter indeed, made it shine, as he brandished it in my eyes; and going to work with an impetuosity and eagerness, bred very likely by a long fast at sea, went to give me a taste of it. I straddled, I humoured my posture, and did my best in short to buckle to it; I took part of it in too, but still things did not go to his thorough liking: changing then in a trice his system of battery, he leads me to the table and with a master-hand lays my head down on the edge of it, and, with the other canting up my petticoats and shift, bares my naked posteriours to his blind and furious guide; it forces its way between them, and I feeling pretty sensibly that it was not going by the right door, and knocking desperately at the wrong one, I told him of it: – "Pooh!" says he, "my dear, any port in a storm." Altering, however, directly his course, and lowering his point, he fixed it right, and driving it up with a delicious stiffness, made all foam again, and gave me the *tout* with such fire and spirit, that in the fine disposition I was in when I submitted to him, and stirr'd up so fiercely as I was, I got the start of him, and went away into the melting swoon, and squeezing him, whilst in the convulsive grasp of it, drew from him such a plenteous bedewal as, join'd to my own effusion, perfectly floated those parts, and drown'd in a deluge all my raging conflagration of desire.

When this was over, how to make my retreat was my concern; for, though I had been so extremely pleas'd with the difference between this warm broadside, pour'd so briskly into me, and the tiresome pawing and toying to which I had owed the unappeas'd flames that had driven me into this step, now I was grown cooler, I began to apprehend the danger of contracting an acquaintance with this, however agreeable, stranger; who, on his side, spoke of passing the evening with me and continuing our intimacy, with an air of determination that made me afraid of its being not so easy to get away from him as I could wish. In the mean time I carefully conceal'd my uneasiness, and readily pretended to consent to stay with him, telling him I should only step to my lodgings to leave a necessary direction, and then instantly return. This he very glibly swallowed, on the notion of my being one of those unhappy street-errants who devote themselves to the pleasure of the first ruffian that will stoop to pick them up, and of course, that I would scarce bilk myself of my hire, by my not returning to make the most of the job. Thus he parted with me, not before, however, he had order'd in my hearing a supper, which I had the barbarity to disappoint him of my company to.

But when I got home and told Mrs. Cole my adventure, she represented so strongly to me the nature and dangerous consequences of my folly, particularly the risks to my health, in being so open-legg'd and free, that I not only took resolutions never to venture so rashly again, which I inviolably preserv'd, but pass'd a good many days in continual uneasiness lest I should have met with other reasons, besides the pleasure of that encounter, to remember it; but these fears wronged my pretty sailor, for which I gladly make him this reparation.

I had now liv'd with Mr. Norbert near a quarter of a year, in which space I circulated my time very pleasantly between my amusements at Mrs. Cole's, and a proper attendance on that gentleman, who paid me profusely for the unlimited complaisance with which I passively humoured every caprice of pleasure, and which had won upon him so greatly, that finding, as he said, all that variety in me alone which he had sought for in a number of women, I had made him lose his taste for inconstancy, and new faces. But what was yet at least agreeable, as well as more flattering, the love I had inspir'd him with bred a deference to me that was of great service to his health: for having by degrees, and with most pathetic representations, brought him to some husbandry of it, and to insure the duration of his pleasures by moderating their use, and correcting those excesses in them he was so addicted to, and which had shatter'd his constitution and destroyed his powers of life in the very point for which he seemed chiefly desirous, to live, he was grown more delicate, more temperate, and in course more healthy; his gratitude for which was taking a turn very favourable for my fortune, when once more the caprice of it dash'd the cup from my lips.

His sister, Lady L——, for whom he had a great affection, desiring him to accompany her down to Bath for her health, he could not refuse her such a favour; and accordingly, though he counted on staying away from me no more than a week at farthest, he took his leave of me with an ominous heaviness of heart, and left me a sum far above the state of his fortune, and very inconsistent with the intended shortness of his journey; but it ended in the longest that can be, and is never but once taken: for, arriv'd at Bath, he was not there two days before he fell into a debauch of drinking with some gentlemen, that threw him into a high fever and carry'd him off in four days time, never once out of a delirium. Had he been in his senses to make a will, perhaps he might have made favourable mention of me in it. Thus, however, I lost him; and as no condition of life is more subject to revolutions than that of a woman of pleasure, I soon recover'd my cheerfulness, and now beheld myself once more struck off the list of kept-mistresses, and returned into the bosom of the community from which I had been in some manner taken.

Mrs. Cole still continuing her friendship, offered me her assistance and advice towards another choice; but I was now in ease and affluence enough to look about me at leisure; and as to any constitutional calls of pleasure, their pressure, or sensibility, was greatly lessen'd by a consciousness of the ease with which they were to be satisfy'd at Mrs. Cole's house, where Louisa and Emily still continu'd in the old way; and by great favourite Harriet used often to come and see me, and entertain me, with her head and heart full of the happiness she enjoy'd with her dear baronet, whom she loved with tenderness, and constancy, even though he was her keeper, and what is yet more, had made her independent, by a handsome provision for her and hers. I was then in this vacancy from any regular employ of my person, in my way of business, when one day, Mrs. Cole, in the course of the constant confidence we lived in, acquainted me that there was one Mr. Barville, who used her house, just come to town, whom she was not a little perplex'd about providing a suitable companion for; which was indeed a point of difficulty, as he was under the tyranny of a cruel taste: that of an ardent desire, not only of being unmercifully whipp'd himself, but of whipping others, in such sort, that tho' he paid extravagantly those who had the courage and complaisance to submit to his humour, there were few, delicate as he was in the choice of his subjects, who would exchange turns with him so terrible at the expense of their skin. But, what yet increased the oddity of this strange fancy was the gentleman being young; whereas it generally attacks, it seems, such as are, through age, obliged to have recourse to this experiment, for quickening the circulation of their sluggish juices, and determining a conflux of the spirits of pleasure towards those flagging, shrivelly parts, that rise to life only by virtue of those titillating ardours created by the discipline of their opposites, with which they have so surprising a consent.

This Mrs. Cole could not well acquaint me with, in any expectation of my offering my service: for, sufficiently easy as I was in my circumstances, it must have been the temptation of an immense interest indeed that could have induced me to embrace such a job; neither had I ever express'd, nor indeed felt, the least impulse or curiosity to know more of a taste that promis'd so much more pain than pleasure to those that stood in no need of such violent goads: what then should move me to subscribe myself voluntarily to a party of pain, foreknowing it such? Why, to tell the plain truth, it was a sudden caprice, a gust of fancy for trying a new experiment, mix'd with the vanity of proving my personal courage to Mrs. Cole, that determined me, at all risks, to propose myself to her, and relieve her from any farther lookout. Accordingly, I at once pleas'd and surpris'd her with a frank and unreserved tender of my person to her, and her friend's absolute disposal on this occasion.

My good temporal mother was, however, so kind as to use all the arguments she could imagine to dissuade me: but, as I found they only turn'd on a motive of tenderness to me, I persisted in my resolution, and thereby acquitted my offer of any suspicion of its not having been sincerely made, or out of compliment only. Acquiescing then thankfully in it, Mrs. Cole assur'd me that bating the pain I should be put to, she had no scruple to engage me to this party, which she assur'd me I should be liberally paid for, and which, the secrecy of the transaction preserved safe from the ridicule that otherwise vulgarly attended it; that for her part, she considered pleasure, of one sort or other, as the universal port of destination, and every wind that blew thither a good one, provided it blew nobody any harm; that she rather compassionated, than blam'd, those unhappy persons who are under a subjection they cannot shake off, to those arbitrary tastes that rule their appetites of pleasures with an unaccountable control: tastes, too, as infinitely diversifi'd, as superior to, and independent of, all reasoning as the different relishes or palates of mankind in their viands, some delicate stomachs nauseating plain meats, and finding no savour but in high-seasoned, luxurious dishes, whilst others again pique themselves upon detesting them.

I stood now in no need of this preamble of encouragement, of justification: my word was given, and I was determin'd to fulfil my engagements. Accordingly the night was set, and I had all the necessary previous instructions how to act and conduct myself. The dining-room was duly prepared and lighted up, and the young gentleman posted there in waiting, for my introduction to him.

I was then, by Mrs. Cole, brought in, and presented to him, in a loose dishabille fitted, by her direction, to the exercise I was to go through, all in the finest linen and a thorough white uniform: gown, petticoat, stockings, and satin slippers, like a victim led to sacrifice; whilst my dark auburn hair, falling in drop-curls over my neck, created a pleasing distinction of colour from the rest of my dress.

As soon as Mr. Barville saw me, he got up, with a visible air of pleasure and surprise, and saluting me, asked Mrs. Cole if it was possible that so fine and delicate a creature would voluntarily submit to such sufferings and rigours as were the subject of his assignation. She answer'd him properly, and now, reading in his eyes that she could not too soon leave us together, she went out, after recommending to him to use moderation with so tender a novice.

But whilst she was employing his attention, mine had been taken up with examining the figure and person of this unhappy young gentleman, who was thus unaccountably condemn'd to have his pleasure lashed into him, as boys have their learning.

He was exceedingly fair, and smooth complexion'd, and appeared to me no more than twenty at most, tho' he was three years older than what my conjectures gave him; but then he ow'd this favourable mistake to a habit of fatness, which spread through a short, squab stature, and a round, plump, fresh-coloured face gave him greatly the look of a Bacchus, had not an air of austerity, not to say sternness, very unsuitable even to his shape of face, dash'd that character of joy, necessary to complete the resemblance. His dress was extremely neat, but plain, and far inferior to the ample fortune he was in full possession of; this too was a taste in him, and not avarice.

As soon as Mrs. Cole was gone, he seated me near him, when now his face changed upon me into an expression of the most pleasing sweetness and good humour, the more remarkable for its sudden shift from the other extreme, which, I found afterwards, when I knew more of his character, was owing to a habitual state of conflict with, and dislike of himself, for being enslaved to so peculiar a gust, by the fatality of a constitutional ascendant, that render'd him incapable of receiving any pleasure till he submitted to these extraordinary means of procuring it at the hands of pain, whilst the constancy of this repining consciousness stamp'd at length that cast of sourness and severity on his features: which was, in fact, very foreign to the natural sweetness of his temper.

After a competent preparation by apologies, and encouragement to go through my part with spirit and constancy, he stood up near the fire, whilst I went to fetch the instruments of discipline out of a closet hard by: these were several rods, made each of two or three strong twigs of birch tied together, which he took, handled, and view'd with as much pleasure, as I did with a kind of shuddering presage.

Next we took from the side of the room a long broad bench, made easy to lie at length on by a soft cushion in a callico-cover; and every thing being now ready, he took his coat and waistcoat off; and at his motion and desire, I unbutton'd his breeches, and rolling up his shirt rather above his waist, tuck'd it in securely there: when directing naturally my eyes to that humoursome master-movement, in whose favour all these dispositions were making, it seemed almost shrunk into his body, scarce shewing its tip above the sprout of hairy curls that cloathed those parts, as you may have seen a wren peep its head out of the grass.

Stooping then to untie his garters, he gave them me for the use of tying him down to the legs of the bench: a circumstance no farther necessary than, as I suppose, it made part of the humour of the thing, since he prescribed it to himself, amongst the rest of the ceremonial.

I led him then to the bench, and according to my cue, play'd at forcing him to lie down: which, after some little shew of reluctance, for form-sake, he submitted to; he was straightway extended flat upon his belly, on the bench, with a pillow under his face; and as he thus tamely lay, I tied him slightly hand and foot, to the legs of it; which done, his shirt remaining truss'd up over the small of his back, I drew his breeches quite down to his knees; and now he lay, in all the fairest, broadest display of that part of the back-view; in which a pair of chubby, smooth-cheek'd and passing white posteriours rose cushioning upwards from two stout, fleshful thighs, and ending their cleft, or separation by an union at the small of the back, presented a bold mark, that swell'd, as it were, to meet the scourge.

Seizing now one of the rods, I stood over him, and according to his direction, gave him in one breath, ten lashes with much good-will, and the utmost nerve and vigour of arm that I could put to them, so as to make those fleshy orbs quiver again under them; whilst he himself seem'd no more concern'd, or to mind them, than a lobster would a fleabite. In the mean time, I viewed intently the effects of them, which to me at least appear'd surprisingly cruel: every lash had skimmed the surface of those white cliffs, which they deeply reddened, and lapping round the side of the furthermost from me, cut specially, into the dimple of it such livid weals, as the blood either spun out from, or stood in large drops on; and, from some of the cuts, I picked out even the splinters of the rod that had stuck in the skin. Nor was this raw work to be wonder'd at, considering the greenness of the twigs and the severity of the infliction, whilst the whole surface of his skin was so smooth-stretched over the hard and firm pulp of flesh that fill'd it, as to yield no play, or elusive swagging under the stroke: which thereby took place the more plum, and cut into the quick.

I was however already so mov'd at the piteous sight, that I

from my heart repented the undertaking, and would willingly have given over, thinking he had full enough; but, he encouraging and beseeching me earnestly to proceed, I gave him ten more lashes; and then resting, survey'd the increase of bloody appearances. And at length, steel'd to the sight by his stoutness in suffering, I continued the discipline, by intervals, till I observ'd him wreathing and twisting his body, in a way that I could plainly perceive was not the effect of pain, but of some new and powerful sensation: curious to dive into the meaning of which, in one of my pauses of intermission, I approached, as he still kept working, and grinding his belly against the cushion under him; and, first stroking the untouched and unhurt side of the flesh-mount next me, then softly insinuating my hand under his thigh, felt the posture things were in forwards, which was indeed surprising: for that machine of his, which I had, by its appearance, taken for an impalpable, or at best a very diminutive subject, was now, in virtue of all that smart and havoc of his skin behind, grown not only to a prodigious stiffness of erection, but to a size that frighted even me: a nonpareil thickness indeed! the head of it alone fill'd the utmost capacity of my grasp. And when, as he heav'd and wriggled to and fro, in the agitation of his strange pleasure, it came into view, it had something of the air of a round fillet of the whitest veal, and like its owner, squob, and short in proportion to its breadth; but when he felt my hand there, he begg'd I would go on briskly with my jerking, or he should never arrive at the last stage of pleasure.

Resuming then the rod and the exercise of it, I had fairly worn out three bundles, when, after an increase of struggles and motion, and a deep sigh or two, I saw him lie still and motionless; and now he desir'd me to desist, which I instantly did; and proceeding to untie him, I could not but be amazed at his passive fortitude, on viewing the skin of his butcher'd, mangled posteriours, late so white, smooth and polish'd, now all one side of them a confused cut-work of weals, livid flesh, gashes and gore, insomuch that when he stood up, he could scarce walk; in short, he was in sweetbriars.

Then I plainly perceived, on the cushion, the marks of a plenteous effusion, and already had his sluggard member run up to its old nestling-place, and enforced itself again, as if ashamed to shew its head; which nothing, it seems, could raise but stripes inflicted on its opposite neighbours, who were thus constantly obliged to suffer for his caprice.

PART IX

My gentleman had now put on his clothes and recomposed himself, when giving me a kiss, and placing me by him, he sat himself down as gingerly as possible, with one side off the cushion, which was too sore for him to bear resting any part of his weight on.

Here he thank'd me for the extreme pleasure I had procured him, and seeing, perhaps, some marks in my countenance of terror and apprehension of retaliation on my own skin, for what I had been the instrument of his suffering in his, he assured me, that he was ready to give up to me any engagement I might deem myself under to stand him, as he had done me, but if that proceeded in my consent to it, he would consider the difference of my sex, its greater delicacy and incapacity to undergo pain. Rehearten'd at which, and piqu'd in honour, as I thought, not to flinch so near the trial, especially as I well knew Mrs. Cole was an eye-witness, from her stand of espial, to the whole of our transactions, I was now less afraid of my skin than of his not furnishing me with an opportunity of signalising my resolution.

Consonant to this disposition was my answer, but my courage was still more in my head, than in my heart; and as cowards rush into the danger they fear, in order to be the sooner rid of the pain of that sensation, I was entirely pleas'd with his hastening matters into execution.

He had then little to do, but to unloose the strings of my petticoats, and lift them, together with my shift, navelhigh, where he just tuck'd them up loosely girt, and might be slipt up higher at pleasure. Then viewing me round with great seeming delight, he laid me at length on my face upon the bench, and when I expected he would tie me, as I had done him, and held out my hands, not without fear and a little trembling, he told me he would by no means terrify me unnecessarily with such a confinement; for that though he meant to put my constancy to some trial, the standing it was to be completely voluntary on my side, and therefore I might be at full liberty to get up whenever I found the pain too much for me. You cannot imagine how much I thought myself bound, by being thus allow'd to remain loose, and how much spirit this confidence in me gave me, so that I was even from my heart careless how much my flesh might suffer in honour of it.

All my back parts, naked half way up, were now fully at his mercy: and first, he stood at a convenient distance, delighting himself with a gloating survey of the attitude I lay in, and of all the secret stores I thus expos'd to him in fair display. Then, springing eagerly towards me, he cover'd all those naked parts with a fond profusion of kisses; and now, taking hold of the rod, rather wanton'd with me, in gentle inflictions on those tender trembling masses of my flesh behind, than in any way hurt them, till by degrees, he began to tingle them with smarter lashes, so as to provoke a red colour into them, which I knew, as well by the flagrant glow I felt there, as by his telling me, they now emulated the native roses of my other cheeks. When he had thus amus'd himself with admiring and toying with them, he went on to strike harder, and more hard; so that I needed all my patience not to cry out, or complain at least. At last, he twigg'd me so smartly as to fetch blood in more than one lash: at sight of which he flung down the rod, flew to me, kissed away the starting drops, and sucking the wounds eased a good deal of my pain. But now raising me on my knees, and making me kneel with them straddling wide, that tender part of me, naturally the province of pleasure, not of pain, came in for its share of suffering: for now, eyeing it wistfully, he directed the rod so that the sharp ends of the twigs lighted there, so sensibly, that I could not help wincing, and writhing my limbs with smart; so that my contortions of body must necessarily throw it into infinite variety of postures and points of view, fit to feast the luxury of the eye. But still I bore every thing without crying out: when presently giving me another pause, he rush'd, as it were, on that part whose lips, and round-about, had felt this cruelty, and by way of reparation, glews his own to them; then he opened, shut, squeez'd them, pluck'd softly the overgrowing moss, and all this in a style of wild passionate rapture and enthusiasm, that express'd excess of pleasure; till betaking himself to the rod again, encourag'd by my passiveness, and infuriated with this strange taste of delight, he made my poor posteriors pay for the ungovernableness of it; for now shewing them no quarter the traitor cut me so, that I wanted but little of fainting away, when he gave over. And yet I did not utter one groan, or angry expostulation; but in heart I resolv'd nothing so seriously, as never to expose myself again to the like serverities.

You may guess then in what a curious pickle those soft flesh-cushions of mine were, all sore, raw, and in fine, terribly clawed off; but so far from feeling any pleasure in it, that the recent smart made me pout a little, and not with the greatest

Fanny Hill Vol II

97

air of satisfaction receive the compliments, and after-caresses of the author of my pain.

As soon as my cloaths were huddled on in a little decency, a supper was brought in by the discreet Mrs. Cole herself, which might have piqued the sensuality of a cardinal, accompanied with a choice of the richest wines: all which she set before us, and went out again, without having, by a word or even by a smile, given us the least interruption or confusion, in those moments of secrecy, that we were not yet ripe to the admission of a third to.

I sat down then, still scarce in charity with my butcher, for such I could not help considering him, and was moreover not a little piqued at the gay, satisfied air of his countenance, which I thought myself insulted by. But when the now necessary refreshment to me of a glass of wine, a little eating (all the time observing a profound silence) had somewhat cheer'd and restor'd me to spirits, and as the smart began to go off, my good humour return'd accordingly: which alteration not escaping him, he said and did everything that could confirm me in, and indeed exalt it.

But scarce was supper well over, before a change so incredible was wrought in me, such violent, yet pleasingly irksome sensations took possession of me that I scarce knew how to contain myself; the smart of the lashes was now converted into such a prickly heat, such fiery tinglings, as made me sigh, squeeze my thighs together, shift and wriggle about my seat, with a furious restlessness; whilst these itching ardours, thus excited in those parts on which the storm of discipline had principally fallen, detach'd legions of burning, subtile, stimulating spirits, to their opposite spot and centre of assemblage, where their titillation rag'd so furiously, that I was even stinging mad with them. No wonder then, that in such a taking, and devour'd by flames that licked up all modesty and reserve, my eyes, now charg'd brimful of the most intense desire, fired on my companion very intelligible signals of distress: my companion, I say, who grew in them every instant more amiable, and more necessary to my urgent wishes and hopes of immediate ease.

Mr. Barville, no stranger by experience to these situations, soon knew the pass I was brought to, soon perceiv'd my extreme disorder; in favour of which, removing the table out of the way, he began a prelude that flatter'd me with instant relief, to which I was not, however, so near as I imagin'd: for as he was unbuttoned to me, and tried to provoke and rouse to action his unactive torpid machine, he blushingly own'd that no good was to be expected from it unless I took it in hand to re-excite its languid loitering powers, by just refreshing the smart of the yet recent blood-raw cuts, seeing it could, no more than a boy's top, keep up without lashing. Sensible then that I should work as much for my own profit as his, I hurried my compliance with his desire, and abridging the ceremonial, whilst he lean'd his head against the back of a chair, I had scarce gently made him feel the lash, before I saw the object of my wishes give signs of life, and presently, as it were with a magic touch, it started up into a noble size and distinction indeed! Hastening then to give me the benefit of it, he threw me down on the bench; but such was the refresh'd soreness of those parts behind, on my leaning so hard on them, as became me to compass the admission of that stupendous head of his machine, that I could not possibly bear it. I got up then, and tried, by leaning forwards and turning the crupper on my assailant, to let him at the back avenue: but here it was likewise impossible to stand his bearing so fiercely against me, in his agitations and endeavours to enter that way, whilst his belly battered directly against the recent sore. What should we do now? both intolerably heated; both in a fury; but pleasure is ever inventive for its own ends: he strips me in a trice, stark naked, and placing a broad settee-cushion on the carpet before the fire, oversets me gently, topsy-turvy, on it; and handling me only at the waist, whilst you may be sure I favour'd all my dispositions, brought my legs round his neck; so that my head was kept from the floor only by my hands and the velvet cushion, which was now bespread with my flowing hair: thus I stood on my head and hands, supported by him in such manner, that whilst my thighs clung round him, so as to expose to his sight all my back figure, including the theatre of his bloody pleasure, the centre of my fore part fairly bearded the object of its rage, that now stood in fine condition to give me satisfaction for the injuries of its neighbours. But as this posture was certainly not the easiest, and our imaginations, wound up to the height, could suffer no delay, he first, with the utmost eagerness and effort, just lip-lodg'd that broad acorn-fashion'd head of his instrument; and still frenzied by the fury with which he had made that impression, he soon stuffed in the rest; when now, with a pursuit of thrusts, fiercely urg'd, he absolutely overpower'd and absorb'd all sense of pain and uneasiness, whether from my wounds behind, my most untoward posture, or the oversize of his stretcher, in an infinitely predominant delight; when now all my whole spirits of life and sensation, rushing impetuously to the cock-pit, where the prize of pleasure was hotly in dispute and clustering to a point there, I soon receiv'd the dear relief of nature from these over-violent strains and provocations of it; harmonizing with which, my gallant spouted into me such a potent overflow of the balsamic injection, as soften'd and unedg'd all those irritating stings of a new species of titillation, which I had been so intolerably madden'd with, and restor'd the ferment of my senses to some degree of composure.

I had now achiev'd this rare adventure ultimately much more to my satisfaction than I had bespoken the nature of it to turn out; nor was it much lessen'd, you may think, by my spark's lavish praises of my constancy and complaisance, which he gave weight to by a present that greatly surpassed my utmost expectation, besides his gratification to Mrs. Cole.

I was not, however, at any time, re-enticed to renew with him, or resort again to the violent expedient of lashing nature into more haste than good speed: which, by the way, I conceive acts somewhat in the manner of a dose of Spanish flies; with more pain perhaps, but less danger; and might be necessary to him, but was nothing less so than to me, whose appetite wanted the bridle more than the spur.

Mrs. Cole, to whom this adventurous exploit had more and more endear'd me, looked on me now as a girl after her own heart, afraid on nothing, and, on a good account, hardy enough to fight all the weapons of pleasure through. Attentive then, in consequence of these favourable conceptions, to promote either my profit or pleasure, she had special regard for the first, in a new gallant of a very singular turn, that she procur'd for and introduced to me.

This was a grave, staid, solemn, elderly gentleman whose peculiar humour was a delight in combing fine tresses of hair; and as I was perfectly headed to his taste, he us'd to come constantly at my *toilette* hours, when I let down my hair as loose as nature, and abandon'd it to him to do what he pleased with it; and accordingly he would keep me an hour or more in play with it, drawing the comb through it, winding the curls round his fingers, even kissing it as he smooth'd it; and all this led to no other use of my person, or any other liberties whatever, any more than if a distinction of sexes had not existed.

Another peculiarity of taste he had, which was to present me with a dozen pairs of the whitest kid gloves at a time: these he would divert himself with drawing on me, and then biting off the fingers' ends; all which fooleries of a sickly appetite, the old gentleman paid more liberally for than most others did for more essential favours. This lasted till a violent cough, seizing and laying him up, deliver'd me from this most innocent and insipid trifler, for I never heard more of him after his first retreat.

You may be sure a by-job of this sort interfer'd with no other pursuit, or plan of life; which I led, in truth, with a modesty and reserve that was less the work of virtue than of exhausted novelty, a glut of pleasure, and easy circumstances, that made me indifferent to any engagements in which pleasure and profit were not eminently united; and such I could, with the less impatience, wait for at the hands of time and fortune, as I was satisfy'd I could never mend my pennyworths, having evidently been serv'd at the top of market, and even been pamper'd with dainties: besides that, in the sacrifice of a few momentary impulses, I found a secret satisfaction in respecting myself, as well as preserving the life and freshness of my complexion. Louisa and Emily did not carry indeed their reserve so high as I did; but still they were far from cheap or abandon'd tho' two of their adventures seem'd to contradict this general character, which, for their singularity, I shall give you in course, beginning first with Emily's:

Louisa and she went one night to a ball, the first in the habit of a shepherdess, Emily in that of a shepherd: I saw them in their dresses before they went, and nothing in nature could represent a prettier boy than this last did, being so fair and well limbed. They had kept together for some time, when

Louisa, meeting an old acquaintance of hers, very cordially gives her companion the drop, and leaves her under the protection of her boy's habit, which was not much, and of her discretion, which was, it seems, still less. Emily, finding herself deserted, sauntered thoughtless about a-while, and, as much for coolness and air as anything else, at length pull'd off her mask and went to the sideboard; where, eyed and mark'd out by a gentleman in a very handsome domino, she was accosted by, and fell into chat with him. The domino, after a little discourse, in which Emily doubtless distinguish'd her good nature and easiness more than her wit, began to make violent love to her, and drawing her insensibly to some benches at the lower end of the masquerade room, for her to sit by him, where he squeez'd her hands, pinch'd her cheeks, prais'd and played with her fine hair, admired her complexion, and all in a style of courtship dash'd with a certain oddity, that not comprehending the mystery of, poor Emily attributed to his falling in with the humour of her disguise; and being naturally not the cruellest of her profession, began to incline to a parley on those essentials. But here was the stress of the joke: he took her really for what she appear'd to be, a smock-fac'd boy; and she, forgetting her dress, and of course ranging quite wide of his ideas, took all those addresses to be paid to herself as a woman, which she precisely owed to his not thinking her one. However, this double error was push'd to such a height on both sides, that Emily, who saw nothing in him but a gentleman of distinction by those points of dress to which his disguise did not extend, warmed too by the wine he had ply'd her with, and the caresses he had lavished upon her, suffered herself to be persuaded to go to a bagnio with him; and thus, losing sight of Mrs. Cole's cautions, with a blind confidence, put herself into his hands, to be carried wherever he pleased. For his part, equally blinded by his wishes, whilst her egregious simplicity favoured his deception more than the most exquisite art could have done, he supposed, no doubt, that he had lighted on some soft simpleton, fit for his purpose, or some kept minion broken to his hand, who understood him perfectly well and enter'd into his designs. But, be that as it would, he led her to a coach, went into it with her, and brought her to a very handsome apartment, with a bed in it; but whether it was a bagnio or not, she could not tell, having spoken to nobody but himself. But when they were alone together, and her *enamorato* began to proceed to those extremities which instantly discover the sex, she remark'd that no description could paint up to the life the mixture of pique, confusion and disappointment that appeared in his countenance, joined to the mournful exclamation: "By heavens, a woman!" This at once opened her eyes, which had hitherto been shut in downright stupidity. However, as if he had meant to retrieve that escape, he still continu'd to toy with and fondle her, but with so staring an alteration from extreme warmth into a chill and forced civility, that even Emily herself could not but take notice of it, and now began to wish she had paid more regard to Mrs. Cole's premonitions against ever engaging with a stranger. And now an excess of timidity succeeded to an excess of confidence, and she thought herself so much at his mercy and discretion, that she stood passive throughout the whole progress of his prelude: for now, whether the impressions of so great a beauty had even made him forgive her her sex, or whether her appearance of figure in that dress still humour'd his first illusion, he recover'd by degrees a good part of his first warmth, and keeping Emily with her breeches still unbuttoned, stript them down to her knees, and gently impelling her to lean down, with her face against the bed-side, placed her so, that the double way, between the double rising behind, presented the choice fair to him, and he was so fairly set on a mis-direction, as to give the girl no small alarms for fear of losing a maidenhead she had not dreamt of. However, her complaints, and a resistance, gentle, but firm, check'd and brought him to himself again; so that turning his steed's head, he drove him at length in the right road, in which his imagination having probably made the most of those resemblances that flatter'd his taste, he got, with much ado, to his journey's end: after which, he led her out himself, and walking with her two or three streets' length, got her a chair, when making her a present not any thing inferior to what she could have expected, he left her, well recommended to the chairman, who, on her directions, brought her home.

This she related to Mrs. Cole and me the same morning, not without the visible remains of the fear and confusion she had been in still stamp'd on her countenance. Mrs. Cole's remark was that her indiscretion proceeding from a constitutional facility, there were little hopes of any thing curing her of it, but repeated severe experience. Mine was that I could not conceive how it was possible for mankind to run into a taste, not only universally odious, but absurd, and impossible to gratify; since, according to the notions and experience I had of things, it was not in nature to force such immense disproportions. Mrs. Cole only smil'd at my ignorance, and said nothing towards my undeception, which was not affected but by ocular demonstration, some months after, which a most singular accident furnish'd me, and which I will here set down, that I may not return again to so disagreeable a subject.

I had, on a visit intended to Harriet, who had taken lodgings at Hampton Court, hired a chariot to go out thither, Mrs. Cole having promis'd to accompany me; but some indispensable business intervening to detain her, I was obliged to set out alone; and scarce had I got a third of my way, before the axle-tree broke down, and I was well off to get out, safe and unhurt, into a publick-house of a tolerable handsome appearance, on the road. Here the people told me that the stage would come by in a couple of hours at farthest; upon which, determining to wait for it, sooner than lose the jaunt I had got so far forward on, I was carried into a very clean decent room, up one pair of stairs, which I took possession of for the time I had to stay, in right of calling for sufficient to do the house justice.

Here, whilst I was amusing myself with looking out of the window, a single horse-chaise stopt at the door, out of which lightly leap'd two gentlemen, for so they seem'd, who came in only as it were to bait and refresh a little, for they gave their horse to be held in readiness against they came out. And presently I heard the door of the next room, where they were let in, and call'd about them briskly; and as soon as they were serv'd, I could just hear that they shut and fastened the door on the inside.

A spirit of curiosity, far from sudden, since I do not know when I was without it, prompted me, without any particular suspicion, or other drift or view, to see what they were, and examine their persons and behaviour. The partition of our rooms was one of those moveable ones that, when taken down, serv'd occasionally to lay them into one, for the conveniency of a large company; and now, my nicest search could not shew me the shadow of a peep-hole, a circumstance which probably had not escap'd the review of the parties on the other side, whom much it stood upon not to be deceived in it; but at length I observed a paper patch of the same colour as the wainscot, which I took to conceal some flaw: but then it was so high, that I was obliged to stand upon a chair to reach it, which I did as softly as possibly, and, with a point of a bodkin, soon pierc'd it. And now, applying my eye close, I commanded the room perfectly, and could see my two young sparks romping and pulling one another about, entirely, to my imagination, in frolic and innocent play.

The eldest might be, on my nearest guess, towards nineteen, a tall comely young man, in a white fustian frock, with a green velvet cape, and a cut bob-wig.

The youngest could not be above seventeen, fair, ruddy, completely well made, and to say the truth, a sweet pretty stripling: he was, I fancy, too, a country-lad, by his dress, which was a green plush frock and breeches of the same, white waistcoat and stockings, a jockey cap, with his yellowish hair, long and loose, in natural curls. But after a look of circumspection, which I saw the eldest cast every way round the room, probably in too much hurry and heat not to overlook the very small opening I was posted at, especially at the height it was, whilst my eye close to it kept the light from shining through and betraying it, he said something to his companion and presently chang'd the face of things.

For now the elder began to embrace, to press and kiss the younger, to put his hands into his bosom, and give him such manifest signs of an amorous intention, as made me conclude the other to be a girl in disguise: a mistake that nature kept me in countenance for, for she had certainly made one, when she gave him the male stamp.

In the rashness then of their age, and bent as they were to accomplish their project of preposterous pleasure, at the risk of the very worst of consequences, where a discovery was nothing less than improbable, they now proceeded to such lengths as soon satisfied me what they were.

For presently the eldest unbuttoned the other's breeches and, removing the linen barrier, brought out to view a white shaft, middle-sized and scarce fledged. When, after handling and playing with it a little, with other dalliance, all received by the boy without other opposition than a certain wayward coyness ten times more alluring than repulsive, he got him to turn round, with his face from him, to a chair that stood hard by. When knowing, I suppose, his office, the Ganymede now obsequiously leaned his head against the back of it, and projecting his body, made a fair mark, still covered with his shirt, as he thus stood in a side-view to me but fronting his companion, who, presently unmasking his battery, produced an engine that certainly deserved to be put to a better use, and very fit to confirm me in my disbelief of the possibility of things being pushed to odious extremities, which I had built on the disproportion of parts. But this disbelief I was now to be cured of, as by my consent all young men should likewise be, that their innocence may not be betrayed into such snares, for want of knowing the extent of their danger; for nothing is more certain than that ignorance of a vice is by no means a guard against it.

Slipping then aside the young lad's shirt, and tucking it up under his clothes behind, he showed to the open air those globular, fleshy eminences that compose the mount-pleasants of Rome, and which now, with all the narrow vale that intersects them, stood displayed and exposed to his attack: nor could I, without a shudder, behold the dispositions he made for it. First then, moistening well with spittle his instrument, obviously to render it glib, he pointed, he introduced it, as I could plainly discern, not only from its direction and my losing sight of it, but by the writhing, twisting, and soft murmured complaints of the young sufferer. But, at length, the first straights of entrance being pretty well got through, everything seemed to move and go pretty currently on, as in a carpet road, without much rub or resistance. And now, passing one hand round his minion's hips, he got hold of his red-topped ivory toy, that stood perfectly stiff, and showed that if he was like his mother behind, he was like his father before; this he diverted himself with, whilst with the other he wantoned with his hair, and leaning forward over his back, drew his face, from which the boy shook the loose curls that fell over it in the posture he stood him in, and brought it towards his, so as to receive a long-breathed kiss, after which, renewing his driving, and thus continuing to harass his rear, the height of the fit came on with its usual symptoms, and dismissed the action.

The criminal scene they acted, I had the patience to see to an end, purely that I might gather more facts and certainly against them in my design to do their deserts instance justice; and accordingly, when they had readjusted themselves, and were preparing to go out, burning as I was with rage and indignation, I jumped down from the chair, in order to raise the house upon them, but with such an unlucky impetuosity, that some nail or ruggedness in the floor caught my foot, and flung me on my face with such violence that I fell senseless on the ground, and must have lain there some time e'er any one came to my relief: so that they, alarmed, I suppose, by the noise of my fall, had more than the necessary time to make a safe retreat. This they effected, as I learnt, with a precipitation nobody could account for, till, when come to myself, and compos'd enough to speak, I acquainted those of the house with the whole transaction I had been evidence to.

When I came home again, and told Mrs. Cole this adventure, she very sensibly observ'd to me that there was no doubt of due vengeance one time or other overtaking these miscreants, however they might escape for the present; and that, had I been the temporal instrument of it, I should have been at least put to a great deal more trouble and confusion that I imagined; that, as to the thing itself, the less said of it was the better; but that though she might be suspected of partiality, from its being the common cause of woman-kind, out of whose mouths this practice tended to take something more than bread, yet she protested against any mixture of passion, with a declaration extorted from her by pure regard to truth; which was that whatever effect this infamous passion had in other ages and other countries, it seem'd a peculiar blessing on our air and climate, that there was a plague-spot visibly imprinted on all that are tainted with it, in this nation at least; for that among numbers of that stamp whom she had known, or at least were universally under the scandalous suspicion of it, she would not name an exception hardly of one of them, whose character was not, in all other respects, the most worthless and despicable that could be, stript of all the manly virtues of their own sex, and fill'd up with only the worst vices and follies of ours: that, in fine, they were scarce less execrable than ridiculous in their monstrous inconsistence, of loathing and condemning women, and all at the same time apeing all their manners, air, lips, skuttle, and, in general, all their little modes of affectation, which become them at least better than they do these unsex'd male misses.

But here, washing my hands of them, I re-plunge into the stream of my history, into which I may very properly ingraft a terrible sally of Louisa's, since I had some share in it myself, and have besides engag'd myself to relate it, in point of countenance to poor Emily. It will add, too, one more example to thousands, in confirmation of the maxim that when women get once out of compass, there are no lengths of licentiousness that they are not capable of running.

One morning then, that both Mrs. Cole and Emily were gone out for the day, and only Louisa and I (not to mention the house-maid) were left in charge of the house, whilst we were loitering away the time in looking through the shop windows, the son of a poor woman, who earned very hard bread indeed by mending stockings, in a stall in the neighbourhood, offer'd us some nosegays, ring'd round a small basket; by selling of which the poor boy eked out his mother's maintenance of them both: nor was he fit for any other way of livelihood, since he was not only a perfect changeling, or idiot, but stammer'd so that there was no understanding even those sounds his halfdozen, at most, animal ideas prompted him to utter.

The boys and servants in the neighbourhood had given him the nick-name of Good-natured Dick, from the soft simpleton's doing everything he was bid at the first word, and from his naturally having no turn to mischief; then, by the way, he was perfectly well made, stout, clean-limb'd, tall of his age, as strong as a horse and, withal, pretty featur'd; so that he was not, absolutely, such a

111

figure to be snuffled at neither, if your nicety could, in favour of such essentials, have dispens'd with a face unwashed, hair tangled for want of combing, and so ragged a plight, that he might have disputed points of shew with e'er a heathen philosopher of them all.

This boy we had often seen, and bought his flowers, out of pure compassion, and nothing more; but just at this time as he stood presenting us his basket, a sudden whim, a start of wayward fancy, seiz'd Louisa; and, without consulting me, she calls him in, and beginning to examine his nosegays, culls out two, one for herself, another for me, and pulling out half a crown, very currently gives it him to change, as if she had really expected he could have changed it: but the boy, scratching his head, made his signs explaining his inability in place of words, which he could not, with all his struggling, articulate.

Louisa, at this, says: "Well, my lad, come up-stairs with me, and I will give you your due," winking at the same time to me, and beckoning me to accompany her, which I did, securing first the street-door, that by this means, together with the shop, became wholly the care of the faithful housemaid.

As we went up, Louisa whispered to me that she had conceiv'd a strange longing to be satisfy'd, whether the general rule held good with regard to this changeling, and how far nature had made him amends, in her best bodily gifts, for her denial of the sublimer intellectual ones; begging, at the same time, my assistance in procuring her this satisfaction. A want of complaisance was never my vice, and I was so far from opposing this extravagant frolic, that now, bit with the same maggot, and my curiosity conspiring with hers, I enter'd plum into it, on my own account.

Consequently, as soon as we came into Louisa's bedchamber, whilst she was amusing him with picking out his nosegays, I undertook the lead, and began the attack. As it was not then very material to keep much measures with a mere natural, I made presently very free with him, though at my first motion of meddling, his surprise and confusion made him receive my advances but awkwardly: nay, insomuch that he bashfully shy'd, and shy'd back a little; till encouraging him with my eyes, plucking him playfully by the hair, sleeking his cheeks, and forwarding my point by a number of little wantonness, I soon turn'd him familiar, and gave nature her sweetest alarm: so that arous'd, and beginning to feel himself, we could, amidst all the innocent laugh and grin I had provoked him into, perceive the fire lighting in his eyes, and, diffusing over his cheeks, blend its glow with that of his blushes. The emotion in short of animal pleasure glar'd distinctly in the simpleton's countenance; yet, struck with the novelty of the scene, he did not know which way to look or move; but tame, passive, simpering, with his mouth half open in stupid rapture, stood and tractably suffer'd me to do what I pleased with him. His basket was dropt out of his hands, which Louisa took care of.

I had now, through more than one rent, discovered and felt his thighs, the skin of which seemed the smoother and fairer for the coarseness, and even dirt of his dress, as the teeth of Negroes seem the whiter for the surrounding black; and poor indeed of habit, poor of understanding, he was, however, abundantly rich in personal treasures, such as flesh, firm, plump, and replete with the juices of youth, and robust well-knit limbs. My fingers too had now got within reach of the true, the genuine sensitive plant, which, instead of shrinking from the touch, joys to meet it, and swells and vegetates under it: mine pleasingly informed me that matters were so ripe for the discovery we meditated, that they were too mighty for the confinement they were ready to break. A waistband that I unskewer'd, and a rag of a shirt that I removed, and which could not have cover'd a quarter of it, revealed the whole of the idiot's standard of distinction, erect, in full pride and display: but such a one! it was positively of so tremendous a size, that prepared as we were to see something extraordinary, it still, out of measure, surpass'd our expectation, and astonish'd even me, who had not been used to trade in trifles. In fine, it might have answered very well the making a show of; its enormous head seemed, in hue and size, not unlike a common sheep's heart; then you might have troll'd dice securely along the broad back of the body of it; the length of it too was prodigious; then the rich appendage of the treasure-bag beneath, large in proportion, gather'd and crisp'd up round in shallow furrows, helped to fill the eye, and complete the proof of his being a natural, not quite in vain; since it was full manifest that he inherited, and largely too, the prerogative of majesty which distinguishes that otherwise most unfortunate condition, and gives rise to the vulgar saying "A fool's bauble is a lady's playfellow." Not wholly without reason: for, generally speaking, it is in love as it is in war, where longest weapon carries it. Nature, in short, had done so much for him in those parts, that she perhaps held herself acquitted in doing so little for his head.

For my part, who had sincerely no intention to push the joke further than simply satisfying my curiosity with the sight of it alone, I was content, in spite of the temptation that star'd me in the face, with having rais'd a May-pole for another to hang a garland on: for, by this time, easily reading Louisa's desires in her wishful eyes, I acted the commodious part and made her, who sought no better sport, significant terms of encouragement to go through-stitch with her adventure; intimating too that I would stay and see fair play: in which, indeed, I had in view to humour a new-born curiosity, to observe what appearances active nature would put on in a natural, in the course of this her darling operation.

Louisa, whose appetite was up, and who, like the industrious bee, was, it seems, not above gathering the sweets of so rare a flower, tho' she found it planted on a dunghill, was but too readily disposed to take the benefit of my cession. Urg'd then strongly by her own desires, and embolden'd by me, she presently determined to risk a trial of parts with the idiot, who was by this time nobly inflam'd for her purpose, by all the irritations we had used to put the principles of pleasure effectually into motion, and to wind up the springs of its organ to their supreme pitch; and it stood accordingly stiff and straining, ready to burst with the blood and spirits that swelled it . . . to a bulk! No! I shall never forget it.

Louisa then, taking and holding the fine handle that so invitingly offer'd itself, led the ductile youth by that master-tool of his, as she stept backward towards the bed; which he joyfully gave way to, under the incitations of instinct and palpably deliver'd up to the goad of desire.

Stopped then by the bed, she took the fall she lov'd, and lean'd to the most, gently backward upon it, still holding fast what she held, and taking care to give her cloaths a convenient toss up, so that her thighs duly disclos'd, and elevated, laid open all the outward prospect of the treasury of love: the rose-lipt overture presenting the cock-pit so fair, that it was not in nature even for a natural to miss it. Nor did he, for Louisa, fully bent on grappling with it, and impatient of dalliance or delay, directed faithfully the point of the battering-piece, and bounded up with a rage of so voracious appetite, to meet and favour the thrust of insertion, that the fierce activity on both sides effected it with such pain of distention, that Louisa cry'd out violently that she was hurt beyond bearing, that she was killed. But it was too late: the storm was up, and force was on her to give way to it; for now the man-machine, strongly work'd upon by the sensual passion, felt so manfully his advantages and superiority, felt withal the sting of pleasure so intolerable, that maddening with it, his joys began to assume a character of furiousness which made me tremble for the too tender Louisa. He seemed, at this juncture, greater than himself; his countenance, before so void of meaning, or expression, now grew big with the importance of the act he was upon. In short, it was not now that he was to be play'd the fool with. But, what is pleasant enough, I myself was aw'd into a sort of respect for him, by the comely terrors his motions dressed him in: his eyes shooting sparks of fire; his face glowing with ardours that gave another life to it; his teeth churning; his whole frame agitated with a raging ungovernable impetuosity: all sensibly betraying the formidable fierceness with which the genial instinct acted upon him. Butting then and goring all before him, and mad and wild like an over-driven steer, he ploughs up the tender furrow, all insensible to Louisa's complaints; nothing can stop, nothing can keep out a fury like his: with which, having once got its head in, its blind rage soon made way for the rest, piercing, rending, and breaking open all obstructions. The torn, split, wounded girl cries, struggles, invokes me to her rescue, and endeavours to get from under the young savage, or shake him off, but alas! in vain: her breath might as soon have still'd or stemm'd a storm in winter, as all her strength have quell'd his rough assault, or put him out of his course. And indeed, all her efforts and struggles were manag'd with such disorder, that they serv'd rather to entangle, and fold her the faster in the twine of his boisterous arms; so that she was tied to the stake, and oblig'd to fight the match out, if she died for it. For his part, instinct-ridden as he was, the expressions of his animal passion, partaking something of ferocity, were rather worrying than kisses, intermix'd with eager ravenous love-bites on her cheeks and neck, the prints of which did not wear out for some days after.

Poor Louisa, however, bore up at length better than could

FANNY HILL VOL II

have been expected; and though she suffer'd, and greatly too, yet, ever true to the good old cause, she suffer'd with pleasure and enjoyed her pain. And soon now, by dint of an enrag'd enforcement, the brute-machine, driven like a whirlwind, made all smoke again, and wedging its way up, to the utmost extremity, left her, in point of penetration, nothing to fear or to desire: and now,

"Gorg'd with the dearest morsel of the earth," (Shakespeare)

Louisa lay, pleas'd to the heart, pleas'd to her utmost capacity of being so, with every fibre in those parts, stretched almost to breaking, on a rack of joy, whilst the instrument of all this overfulness searched her senses with its sweet excess, till the pleasure gained upon her so, its point stung her so home, that catching at length the rage from her furious driver and sharing the riot of his wild rapture, she went wholly out of her mind into that favourite part of her body, the whole intenseness of which was so fervously fill'd, and employ'd: there alone she existed, all lost in those delirious transports, those ecstasies of the senses, which her winking eyes, the brighten'd vermilion of her lips and cheeks, and sighs of pleasure deeply fetched, so pathetically express'd. In short, she was now as mere a machine as much wrought on, and had her motions as little at her own command as the natural himself, who thus broke in upon her, made her feel with a vengeance his tempestuous tenderness, and the force of the mettle he battered with; their active loins quivered again with the violence of their conflict, till the surge of pleasure, foaming and raging to a height, drew down the pearly shower that was to allay this hurricane. The purely sensitive idiot then first shed those tears of joy that attend its last moments, not without an agony of delight and even almost a roar of rapture, as the gush escaped him; so sensibly too for Louisa, that she kept him faithful company, going off, in consent, with the old symptoms: a delicious delirium, a tremulous convulsive shudder, and the critical dying 'Oh!' And now, on his getting off, she lay pleasure-drench'd, and re-gorging its essential sweets; but quite spent, and gasping for breath, without other sensation of life than in those exquisite vibrations that trembled yet on the strings of delight, which had been too intensively touched, and which nature had been too intensely stirred with, for the senses to be quickly at peace from.

As for the changeling, whose curious engine had been thus successfully played off, his shift of countenance and gesture had even something droll, or rather tragi-comic in it: there was now an air of sad repining foolishness, superadded to his natural one of no-meaning and idiotism, as he stood with his label of manhood, now lank, unstiffen'd, becalm'd, and flapping against his thighs, down which it reach'd half-way, terrible even in its fall, whilst under the dejection of spirit and flesh, which naturally followed, his eyes, by turns, cast down towards his struck standard, or piteously lifted to Louisa, seemed to require at her hands what he had so sensibly parted from to her, and now ruefully miss'd. But the vigour of nature, soon returning, dissipated the blast of faintness which the common law of enjoyment had subjected him to; and now his basket re-became his main concern, which I look'd for, and brought him, whilst Louisa restor'd his dress to its usual condition, and afterwards pleased him perhaps more by taking all his flowers off his hands, and paying him, at his rate, for them, than if she had embarrass'd him by a present that he would have been puzzled to account for, and might have put others on tracing the motives of.

Whether she ever return'd to the attack I know not, and, to say the truth, I believe not. She had had her freak out, and had pretty plentifully drown'd her curiosity in a glut of pleasure, which, as it happened, had no other consequence than that the lad, who retain'd only a confused memory of the transaction, would, when he saw her, for some time after, express a grin of joy and familiarity, after his idiot manner, and soon forgot her in favour of the next woman, tempted, on the report of his parts, to take him in.

PART X

Louisa herself did not long outstay this adventure at Mrs. Cole's (to whom, by-the-by, we took care not to boast of our exploit, till all fear of consequences were clearly over): for an occasion presenting itself of proving her passion for a young fellow, at the expense of her discretion, proceeding all in character, she pack'd up her toilet at half a day's warning and went with him abroad, since which I entirely lost sight of her, and it never fell in my way to hear what became of her.

But a few days after she had left us, two very pretty young gentlemen, who were Mrs. Cole's especial favourites, and free of her academy, easily obtain'd her consent for Emily's and my acceptance of a party of pleasure at a little but agreeable house belonging to one of them, situated not far up the river Thames, on the Surrey side.

Everything being settled, and it being a fine summerday, but rather of the warmest, we set out after dinner, and got to our *rendez-vous* about four in the afternoon; where, landing at the foot of a neat, joyous pavillion, Emily and I were handed into it by our squires, and there drank tea with a cheerfulness and gaiety that the beauty of the prospect, the serenity of the weather, and the tender politeness of our sprightly gallants naturally led us into.

After tea, and taking a turn in the garden, my particular, who was the master of the house, and had in no sense schem'd this party of pleasure for a dry one, propos'd to us, with that frankness which his familiarity at Mrs. Cole's entitled him to, as the weather was excessively hot, to bathe together, under a commodious shelter that he had prepared expressly for that purpose, in a creek of the river, with which a side-door of the pavilion immediately communicated, and where we might be sure of having our diversion out, safe from interruption, and with the utmost privacy.

Emily, who never refus'd anything, and I, who ever delighted in bathing, and had no exception to the person who propos'd it, or to those pleasures it was easy to guess it implied, took care, on this occasion, not to wrong our training at Mrs. Cole's, and agreed to it with as good a grace as we could. Upon which, without loss of time, we return'd instantly to the pavilion, one door of which open'd into a tent, pitch'd before it, that with its marquise, formed a pleasing defense against the sun, or the weather, and was besides as private as we could wish. The lining of it, imbossed cloth, represented a wild forest-foliage, from the top down to the sides, which, in the same stuff, were figur'd with fluted pilasters, with their spaces between fill'd with flower-vases, the whole having a gay effect upon the eye, wherever you turn'd it.

Then it reached sufficiently into the water, yet contain'd convenient benches round it, on the dry ground, either to keep our cloaths, or – , or – , in short, for more uses than resting upon. There was a side-table too, loaded with sweetmeats, jellies, and other eatables, and bottles of wine and cordials, by way of occasional relief from any rawness, or chill of the water, or from any faintness from whatever cause; and in fact, my gallant, who understood *chere entière* perfectly, and who, for taste (even if you would not approve this specimen of it) might have been comptroller of pleasures to a Roman emperor, had left no requisite towards convenience or luxury unprovided.

As soon as we had look'd round this inviting spot, and every preliminary of privacy was duly settled, strip was the word: when the young gentlemen soon dispatch'd the undressing each his partner and reduced us to the naked confession of all those secrets of person which dress generally hides, and which the discovery of was, naturally speaking, not to our disadvantage. Our hands, indeed, mechanically carried towards the most interesting part of us, screened, at first, all from the tufted cliff downwards, till we took them away at their desire, and employed them in doing them the same office, of helping off with their cloaths; in the process of which, there pass'd all the little wantonnesses and frolicks that you may easily imagine.

As for my spark, he was presently undressed, all to his shirt, the fore-lappet of which as he lean'd languishingly on me, he smilingly pointed to me to observe, as it bellied out, or rose and fell, according to the unruly starts of the motion behind it; but it was soon fix'd, for now taking off his shirt, and naked as a Cupid, he shew'd it me at so upright a stand, as prepar'd me indeed for his application to me for instant ease; but, tho' the sight of its fine size was fit enough to fire me, the cooling air, as I stood in this state of nature, joined to the desire I had of bathing first, enabled me to put him off, and tranquillize him, with the remark that a little suspense would only set a keener edge on the pleasure. Leading then the way, and shewing our friends an example of continency, which they were giving signs of losing respect to, we went hand in hand into the stream, till it took us up to our neck, where the no more than grateful coolness of the water gave my senses a delicious refreshment from the sultriness of the season, and made more alive, more happy in myself, and, in course, more alert, and open to voluptuous impressions.

Here I lav'd and wanton'd with the water, or sportively play'd with my companion, leaving Emily to deal with hers at discretion. Mine, at length, not content with making me take the plunge over head and ears, kept splashing me, and provoking me with all the little playful tricks he could devise, and which I strove not to remain in his debt for. We gave, in short, a loose to mirth; and now, nothing would serve him but giving his hands the regale of going over every part of me, neck, breast, belly, thighs, and all the *et cetera*, so dear to the imagination, under the pretext of washing and rubbing them; as we both stood in the water, no higher now than the pit of our stomachs, and which did not hinder him from feeling, and toying with that leak that distinguishes our sex, and it so wonderfully water-tight: for his fingers, in vain dilating and opening it, only let more flame than water into it, be it said without a figure. At the same time he made me feel his own engine, which was so well wound up, as to stand even the working in water, and he accordingly threw one arm round my neck, and was endeavouring to get the better of that harsher construction bred by the surrounding fluid; and had in effect won his way so far as to make me sensible of the pleasing stretch of those nether-lips, from the in-driving machine; when, independent of my not liking that awkward mode of enjoyment, I could not help interrupting him, in order to become joint spectators of a plan of joy, in hot operation between Emily and her partner; who impatient of the fooleries and dalliance of the bath, had led his nymph to one of the benches on the green bank, where he was very cordially proceeding to teach her the difference betwixt jest and earnest.

There, setting her on his knee, and gliding one hand over the surface of that smooth polish'd snow-white skin of hers, which now doubly shone with a dew-bright lustre, and presented to the touch something like what one would imagine of animated ivory, especially in those ruby-nippled globes, which the touch is so fond of and delights to make love to, with the other he was lusciously exploring the sweet secret of nature, in order to make room for a stately piece of machinery, that stood uprear'd, between her thighs, as she continued sitting on his lap, and pressed hard for instant admission, which the tender Emily, in a fit of humour deliciously protracted, affecting to decline, and elude the very pleasure she sigh'd for, but in a style of waywardness so prettily put on, and managed, as to render it ten times more poignant; then her eyes, all amidst the softest dying languishment, express'd at once a mock denial and extreme desire, whilst her sweetness was zested with a coyness so pleasingly provoking, her moods of keeping him off were so attractive, that they redoubled the impetuous rage with which he cover'd her with kisses: and the kisses that, whilst she seemed to shy from or scuffle for, the cunning wanton contrived such sly returns of, as were doubtless the sweeter for the gust she gave them, of being stolen ravished.

Thus Emily, who knew no art but that which nature itself, in favour of her principal end, pleasure, had inspir'd her with, the art of yielding, coy'd it indeed, but coy'd it to the purpose; for with all her straining, her wrestling, and striving to break from the clasp of his arms, she was so far wiser yet than to mean it, that in her struggles, it was visible she aim'd at nothing more than multiplying points of touch with him, and drawing yet closer the folds that held them every where entwined, like two tendrils of a vine intercurling together: so that the same effect, as when Louisa strove in good earnest to disengage from the idiot, was now produced by different motives.

Mean while, their emersion out of the cold water had caused a general glow, a tender suffusion of heighten'd carnation over their bodies; both equally white and smoothskinned; so that as their limbs were thus amorously interwoven, in sweet confusion, it was scarce possible to distinguish who they respectively belonged to, but for the brawnier, bolder muscles of the stronger sex.

In a little time, however, the champion was fairly in with her, and had tied at all points the true lover's knot; when now, adieu all the little refinements of a finessed reluctance; adieu the friendly feint! She was presently driven forcibly out of the power of using any art; and indeed, what art must not give way, when nature, corresponding with her assailant, invaded in the heart of her capital and carried by storm, lay at the mercy of the proud conqueror who had made his entry triumphantly and completely? Soon, however, to become a tributary: for the engagement growing hotter and hotter, at close quarters, she presently brought him to the pass of paying down the dear debt to nature; which she had no sooner collected in, but, like a duellist who has laid his

THE SCARLET LIBRARY

antagonist at his feet, when he has himself received a mortal wound, Emily had scarce time to plume herself upon her victory, but, shot with the same discharge, she, in a loud expiring sigh, in the closure of her eyes, the stretch-out of her limbs, and a remission of her whole frame, gave manifest signs that all was as it should be.

For my part, who had not with the calmest patience stood in the water all this time, to view this warm action, I lean'd tenderly on my gallant, and at the close of it, seemed to ask him with my eyes what he thought of it; but he, more eager to satisfy me by his actions than by words or looks, as we shoal'd the water towards the shore, shewed me the staff of love so intensely set up, that had not even charity beginning at home in this case, urged me to our mutual relief, it would have been cruel indeed to have suffered the youth to burst with straining, when the remedy was so obvious and so near at hand.

Accordingly we took to a bench, whilst Emily and her spark, who belonged it seems to the sea, stood at the sideboard, drinking to our good voyage: for, as the last observ'd, we were well under weigh, with a fair wind up channel, and full-freighted; nor indeed were we long before we finished our trip to Cythera, and unloaded in the old haven; but, as the circumstances did not admit of much variation, I shall spare you the description.

At the same time, allow me to place you here an excuse I am conscious of owing you, for having, perhaps, too much affected the figurative style; though surely, it can pass nowhere more allowably than in a subject which is so properly the province of poetry, nay, is poetry itself, pregnant with every flower of imagination and loving metaphors, even were not the natural expressions, for respects of fashion and sound, necessarily forbid it.

Resuming now my history, you may please to know that

what with a competent number of repetitions, all in the same strain (and, by-the-by, we have a certain natural sense that those repetitions are very much to the taste), what with a circle of pleasures delicately varied, there was not a moment lost to joy all the time we staid there, till late in the night we were re-escorted home by our squires, who delivered us safe to Mrs. Cole, with generous thanks for our company.

This too was Emily's last adventure in our way: for scarce a week after, she was, by an accident too trivial to detail to you the particulars, found out by her parents, who were in good circumstances, and who had been punish'd for their partiality to their son, in the loss of him, occasion'd by a circumstance of their over-indulgence to his appetite; upon which the so long engross'd stream of fondness, running violently in favour of this lost and inhumanly abandon'd child whom if they had not neglected enquiry about, they might long before have recovered. They were now so overjoyed at the retrieval of her, that, I presume, it made them much less strict in examining the bottom of things: for they seem'd very glad to take for granted, in the lump, everything that the grave and decent Mrs. Cole was pleased to pass upon them; and soon afterwards sent her, from the country, a handsome acknowledgement.

But it was not so easy to replace to our community the loss of so sweet a member of it: for, not to mention her beauty, she was one of those mild, pliant characters that if one does not entirely esteem, one can scarce help loving, which is not such a bad compensation neither. Owing all her weakness to good-nature, and an indolent facility that kept her too much at the mercy of first impressions, she had just sense enough to know that she wanted leading-strings, and thought herself so much obliged to any who would take the pains to think for her, and guide her, that with a very little management, she was capable of being made a most agreeable, nay, a most virtuous wife: for vice, it is probable, had never been her choice, or her fate, if it had not been for occasion, or example, or had she not depended less upon herself than upon her circumstances. This presumption her conduct afterwards verified: for presently meeting with a match that was ready cut and dry for her, with a neighbour's son of her own rank, and a young man of sense and order, who took her as the widow of one lost at sea (for so it seems one of her gallants, whose name she had made free with, really was), she naturally struck into all the duties of their domestic life with as much constancy and regularity, as if she had never swerv'd from a state of undebauch'd innocence from her youth.

These desertions had, however, now so far thinned Mrs. Cole's brood that she was left with only me like a hen with one chicken; but tho' she was earnestly entreated and encourag'd to recruit her *corps*, her growing infirmities, and, above all, the tortures of a stubborn hip-gout, which she found would yield to no remedy, determin'd her to bread up her business and retire with a decent pittance into the country, where I promis'd myself nothing so sure, as my going down to live with her as soon as I had seen a little more of life and improv'd my small matters into a competency that would create in me an independence on the world: for I was, now, thanks to Mrs. Cole, wise enough to keep that essential in view.

Thus was I then to lose my faithful preceptress, as did the philosophers of the town the white crow of her profession. For besides that she never ransacked her customers, whose taste too she ever studiously consulted, besides that she never racked her pupils with unconscionable extortions, nor ever put their hard earnings, as she call'd them, under the contribution of poundage. She was a severe enemy to the seduction for innocence, and confin'd her acquisitions solely to those unfortunate young women, who, having lost it, were but the juster objects of compassion: among these, indeed, she pick'd but such as suited her views and taking them under her protection, rescu'd them from the danger of the publick sinks of ruin and misery, to place, or do for them, well or ill, in the manner you have seen. Having then settled her affairs, she set out on her journey, after taking the most tender leave of me, and at the end of some excellent instructions, recommending me to myself, with an anxiety perfectly maternal. In short, she affected me so much, that I was not presently reconcil'd to myself for suffering her at any rate to go without me; but fate had, it seems, otherwise dispos'd of me.

I had, on my separation from Mrs. Cole, taken a pleasant convenient house at Marylebone, but easy to rent and manage from its smallness, which I furnish'd neatly and modestly. There, with a reserve of eight hundred pounds, the fruit of my deference to Mrs. Cole's counsels, exclusive of cloaths, some jewels, some plate, I saw myself in purse for a long time, to wait without impatience for what the chapter of accidents might produce in my favour.

Here, under the new character of a young gentle-woman whose husband was gone to sea, I had mark'd me out such lines of life and conduct, as leaving me at a competent liberty to pursue my views either out of pleasure or fortune, bounded me nevertheless strictly within the rules of decency and discretion: a disposition in which you cannot escape observing a true pupil of Mrs. Cole.

I was scarce, however, well warm in my new abode, when going out one morning pretty early to enjoy the freshness of it, in the pleasing outlet of the fields, accompanied only by a maid, whom I had newly hired, as we were carelessly walking among the trees we were alarmed with the noise of a violent coughing: turning our heads towards which, we distinguish'd a plain well-dressed elderly gentleman, who, attack'd with a sudden fit, was so much overcome as to be forc'd to give way to it and sit down at the foot of a tree, where he seemed suffocating with the severity of it, being perfectly black in the face: not less mov'd than frighten'd with which, I flew on the instant to his relief, and using the rote of practice I had observ'd on the like occasion, I loosened his cravat and clapped him on the back; but whether to any purpose, or whether the cough had had its course, I know not, but the fit immediately went off; and now recover'd to his speech and legs, he returned me thanks with as much emphasis as if I had sav'd his life. This naturally engaging a conversation, he acquainted me where he lived, which was at a considerable distance from where I met with him, and where he had stray'd insensibly on the same intention of a morning walk.

He was, as I afterwards learn'd in the course of the intimacy which this little accident gave birth to, an old bachelor, turn'd of sixty, but of a fresh vigorous complexion, insomuch that he scarce marked five and forty, having never rack'd his constitution by permitting his desires to overtax his ability.

As to his birth and condition, his parents, honest and fail'd mechanics, had, by the best traces he could get of them, left him an infant orphan on the parish; so that it was from a charity-school, that, by honesty and industry, he made his way into a merchant's counting-house; from whence, being sent to a house in Cadiz, he there, by his talents and activity, acquired a fortune, but an immense one, with which he returned to his native country; where he could not, however, so much as fish out one single relation out of the obscurity he was born in. Taking then a taste for retirement, and pleas'd to enjoy life, like a mistress in the dark, he flowed his days in all the ease of opulence, without the least parade of it; and, rather studying the concealment than the shew of a fortune, looked down on a world he perfectly knew; himself, to his wish, unknown and unmarked by.

But, as I propose to devote a letter entirely to the pleasure of retracing to you all the particulars of my acquaintance with this ever, to me, memorable friend, I shall, in this, transiently touch on no more than may serve, as mortar to cement, to form the connection of my history, and to obviate your surprise that one of my high blood and relish of life should count a gallant of threescore such a catch.

Referring then to a more explicit narrative, to explain by what progressions our acquaintance, certainly innocent at first, insensibly changed nature, and ran into unplatonic lengths, as might well be expected from one of my condition of life, and above all, from that principle of electricity that scarce ever fails of producing fire when the sexes meet. I shall only her acquaint you, that as age had not subdued his tenderness for our sex, neither had it robbed him of the power of pleasing, since whatever he wanted in the bewitching charms of youth, he aton'd for, or supplemented with the advantages of experience, the sweetness of his manners, and above all, his flattering address in touching the heart, by an application to the understanding. From him it was I first learn'd, to any purpose, and not without infinite pleasure, that I had such a portion of me worth bestowing some regard on; from him I received my first essential encouragement, and instructions how to put it in that train of cultivation, which I have since pushed to the little degree of improvement you see it at; he it was, who first taught me to be sensible that the pleasures of the mind were superior to those of the body; at the same time, that they were so far from obnoxious to, or incompatible with each other, that, besides the sweetness in the variety and transition, the one serv'd to exalt and perfect the taste of the other to a degree that the senses alone can never arrive at.

Himself a rational pleasurist, as being much too wise to be asham'd of the pleasures of humanity, loved me indeed, but loved me with dignity; in a mean equally remov'd from the sourness, of forwardness, by which age is unpleasingly characteriz'd, and from that childish silly dotage that so often disgraces it, and which he himself used to turn into ridicule, and compare to an old goat affecting the frisk of a young kid.

In short, everything that is generally unamiable in his season of life was, in him, repair'd by so many advantages, that he existed a proof, manifest at least to me, that it is not out of the power of age to please, if it lays out to please, and if, making just allowances, those in that class do not forget that it must cost them more pains and attention than what youth, the natural spring-time of joy, stands in need of: as fruits out of season require proportionably more skill and cultivation, to force them.

With this gentleman then, who took me home soon after our acquaintance commenc'd, I lived near eight months; in which time, my constant complaisance and docility, my attention to deserve his confidence and love, and a conduct, in general, devoid of the least art and founded on my sincere regard and esteem for him, won and attach'd him so firmly to me, that, after having generously trusted me with a genteel, independent settlement, proceeding to heap marks of affection on me, he appointed me, by an authentic will, his sole heiress and executrix: a disposition which he did not outlive two months, being taken from me by a violent cold that he contracted as he unadvisedly ran to the window on an alarm of fire, at some streets distance, and stood there naked-breasted, and exposed to the fatal impressions of a damp night-air.

After acquitting myself of my duty towards my deceas'd benefactor, and paying him a tribute of unfeign'd sorrow, which a little time chang'd into a most tender, grateful memory of him that I shall ever retain, I grew somewhat comforted by the prospect that now open'd to me, if not of happiness at least of affluence and independence.

I saw myself then in the full bloom and pride of youth (for I was not yet nineteen) actually at the head of so large a fortune, as it would have been even the height of impudence in me to have raised my wishes, much more my hopes, to; and that this unexpected elevation did not turn my head, I ow'd to the pains my benefactor had taken to form and prepare me for it, as I ow'd his opinion of my management of the vast possessions he left me, to what he had observ'd of the prudential economy I had learned under Mrs. Cole, of which the reserve he saw I had made was a proof and encouragement to him.

But, alas! how easily is the enjoyment of the greatest sweets in life, in present possession, poisoned by the regret of an absent one! but my regret was a mighty and just one, since it had my only truly beloved Charles for its object.

Given him up I had, indeed, completely, having never once heard from him since our separation; which, as I found afterwards, had been my misfortune, and not his neglect, for he wrote me several letters which had all miscarried; but forgotten him I never had. Amidst all my personal infidelities, not one had made a pin's point impression on a heart impenetrable to the true love-passion, but for him.

As soon, however, as I was mistress of this unexpected fortune, I felt more than ever how dear he was to me, from its insufficiency to make me happy, whilst he was not to share it with me. My earliest care, consequently, was to endeavour at getting some account of him; but all my researches produc'd me no more light than that his father had been dead for some time, not so well as even with the world; and that Charles had reached his port of destination in the South-Seas, where, finding the estate he was sent to recover dwindled to a trifle, by the loss of two ships in which the bulk of his uncle's fortune lay, he was come away with the small remainder, and might, perhaps, according to the best advice, in a few months return to England, from whence he had, at the time of this my inquiry, been absent two years and seven months. A little eternity in love!

You cannot conceive with what joy I embraced the hopes thus given me of seeing the delight of my heart again. But, as the term of months was assigned it, in order to divert and amuse my impatience for his return, after settling my affairs with much ease and security, I set out on a journey for Lancashire, with an equipage suitable to my fortune, and with a design purely to revisit my place of nativity, for which I could not help retaining a great tenderness; and might naturally not be sorry to shew myself there, to the advantage I was now in pass to do, after the report Esther Davis had spread of my being spirited away to the plantations; for on no other supposition could she account for the suppression of myself to her, since her leaving me so abruptly at the inn. Another favourite intention I had, to look out for my relations, though I had none besides distant ones, and prove a benefactress to them. Then Mrs. Cole's place of retirement lying in my way, was not amongst the least of the pleasures I had proposed to myself in this expedition.

I had taken nobody with me but a discreet decent woman, to figure it as my companion, besides my servants, and was scarce got into an inn, about twenty miles from London, where I was to sup and pass the night, when such a storm of wind and rain sprang up as made me congratulate myself on having got under shelter before it began.

This had continu'd a good half hour, when bethinking me of some directions to be given to the coachman, I sent for him, and not caring that his shoes should soil the very clean parlour, in which the cloth was laid, I stept into the hallkitchen, where he was, and where, whilst I was talking to him, I slantingly observ'd two horsemen driven in by the weather, and both wringing wet; one of whom was asking if they could not be assisted with a change, while their clothes were dried. But, heavens! who can express what I felt at the sound of a voice, ever present to my heart, and that is now rebounded at! or when pointing my eyes towards the person it came from, they confirm'd its information, in spite of so long an absence, and of a dress one would have imagin'd studied for a disguise: a horseman's great coat, with a stand-up cape, and his hat flapp'd – but what could escape the piercing alertness of a sense surely guided by love? A transport then like mine was above all consideration, or schemes of surprise; and I, that instant, with the rapidity of the emotions that I felt the spur of, shot into his arms, crying out, as I threw mine round his neck: "My life! – my soul! – my Charles! – " and without further power of speech, swoon'd away, under the pressing agitations of joy and surprise.

Recover'd out of my entrancement, I found myself in my charmer's arms, but in the parlour, surrounded by a crowd which this event had gather'd round us, and which immediately, on a signal from the discreet landlady, who currently took him for my husband, clear'd the room, and desirably left us alone to the raptures of this reunion; my joy at which had like to have prov'd, at the expense of my life, power superior to that of grief at our fatal separation.

The first object then, that my eyes open'd on, was their supreme idol, and my supreme wish Charles, on one knee, holding me fast by the hand and gazing on me with a transport of fondness. Observing my recovery, he attempted to speak, and give vent to his patience of hearing my voice again, to satisfy him once more that it was me; but the mightiness and suddenness of the surprise, continuing to stun him, choked his utterance: he could only stammer out a few broken, half formed, faltering accents, which my ears greedily drinking in, spelt, and put together, so as to make out their sense; "After so long! – so cruel – an absence! – my dearest Fanny! – can it? – can it be you? – " stifling me at the same time with kisses, that, stopping my mouth, at once prevented the answer that he panted for, and increas'd the delicious disorder in which all my senses were rapturously lost. Amidst however, this crowd of ideas, and all blissful ones, there obtruded only one cruel doubt, that poison'd nearly all the transcendent happiness: and what was it, but my dread of its being too excessive to be real? I trembled now with the fear of its being no more than a dream, and of my waking out of it into the horrors of finding it one. Under this fond apprehension, imagining I could not make too much of the present prodigious joy, before it should vanish and leave me in the desert again, nor verify its reality too strongly, I clung to him, I clasp'd him, as if to hinder him from escaping me again: "Where have you been? – how could you – could you leave me? – Say you are still mine – that you still love me – and thus! thus!" (kissing him as if I would consolidate lips with him!) "I forgive you – forgive my hard fortune in favour of this restoration."

All these interjections breaking from me, in that wildness of expression that justly passes for eloquence in love, drew from him all the returns my fond heart could wish or require. Our caresses, our questions, our answers, for some time observ'd no order; all crossing, or interrupting one another in sweet confusion, whilst we exchang'd hearts at our eyes, and renew'd the ratifications of a love unbated by time or absence: not a breath, not a motion, not a gesture on either side, but what was strongly impressed with it. Our hands, lock'd in each other, repeated the most passionate squeezes, so that their fiery thrill went to the heart again.

Thus absorbed, and concentre'd in this unutterable delight, I had not attended to the sweet author of it, being thoroughly wet, and in danger of catching cold; when, in good time, the landlady, whom the appearance of my equipage (which, by-the-by, Charles knew nothing of) had gain'd me an interest in, for me and mine, interrupted us by bringing in a decent shift of linen and cloaths, which now, somewhat recover'd into a calmer composure by the coming in of a third person, I prest him to take the benefit of, with a tender concern and anxiety that made me tremble for his health.

The landlady leaving us again, he proceeded to shift; in the act of which, tho' he proceeded with all that modesty which became these first solemner instants of our re-meeting after so long an absence, I could not contain certain snatches of my eyes, lured by the dazzling discoveries of his naked skin, that escaped him as he chang'd his linen, and which I could not observe the unfaded life and complexion of without emotions of tenderness and joy, that had himself too purely for their object to partake of a loose or mistim'd desire.

He was soon drest in these temporary cloaths, which neither fitted him nor became the light my passion plac'd him in, to me at least; yet, as they were on him, they look'd extremely well, in virtue of that magic charm which love put into everything that he touch'd, or had relation to him: and where, indeed, was that dress that a figure like this would not give grace to? For now, as I ey'd him more in detail, I could not but observe the even favourable alteration which the time of his absence had produced in his person.

There were still the requisite lineaments, still the same vivid vermilion and bloom reigning in his face: but now the roses were more fully blown; the tan of his travels, and a beard somewhat more distinguishable, had, at the expense of no more delicacy than what he could well spare, given it an air of becoming manliness and maturity, that symmetris'd nobly with that air of distinction and empire with which nature had stamp'd it, in a rare mixture with the sweetness of it; still nothing had he lost of that smooth plumpness of flesh, which, glowing with freshness, blooms florid to the eye, and delicious to the touch; then his shoulders were grown more square, his shape more form'd, more portly, but still free and airy. In short, his figure show'd riper, greater, and perfecter to the experienced eye than in his tender youth; and now he was not much more than two and twenty.

In this interval, however, I pick'd out of the broken, often pleasingly interrupted account of himself, that he was, at that instant, actually on his road to London, in not a very paramount plight or condition, having been wreck'd on the Irish coast for which he had prematurely embark'd, and lost the little all he had brought with him from the South Seas; so that he had not till after great shifts and hardships, in the company of his fellow-traveller, the captain, got so far on his journey; that so it was (having heard of his father's death and circumstances) he had now the world to begin again, on a new account: a situation which he assur'd me, in a vein of sincerity that, flowing from his heart, penetrated mine, gave him to farther pain, than that he had it not in his power to make me as happy as he could wish. My fortune, you will please to observe, I had not enter'd upon any overture of, reserving to feast myself with the surprise of it to him, in calmer instants. And, as to my dress, it could give him no idea of the truth, not only as it was mourning, but likewise in a style of plainness and simplicity that I had ever kept to with studied art. He press'd me indeed tenderly to satisfy his ardent curiosity, both with regard to my past and present state of life since his being torn away from me: but I had the address to elude his questions by answers that, shewing his satisfaction at no great distance, won upon him to waive his impatience, in favour of the thorough confidence he had in my not delaying it, but for respects I should in good time acquaint him with.

Charles, however, thus returned to my longing arms, tender, faithful, and in health, was already a blessing too mighty for my conception: but Charles in distress! . . . Charles reduc'd, and broken down to his naked personal merit, was such a circumstance, in favour of the sentiments I had for him, as exceeded my utmost desires; and accordingly I seemed so visibly charm'd, so out of time and measure pleas'd at his mention of his ruin'd fortune, that he could account for it no way, but that the joy of seeing him again had swallow'd up every other sense, or concern.

In the mean time, my woman had taken all possible care of Charles's travelling companion; and as supper was coming in, he was introduc'd to me, when I receiv'd him as became my regard for all of Charles's acquaintance or friends.

We four then supp'd together, in the style of joy, congratulation, and pleasing disorder that you may guess. For my part, though all these agitations had left me not the least stomach but for that uncloying feast, the sight of my ador'd youth, I endeavour'd to force it, by way of example for him, who I conjectur'd must want such a recruit after riding; and, indeed, he ate like a traveller, but gaz'd at, and addressed me all the time like a lover.

After the cloth was taken away, and the hour of repose came on, Charles and I were, without further ceremony, in quality of man and wife, shewn up together to a very handsome apartment, and, all in course, the bed, they said, the best in the inn.

And here, Decency, forgive me! if once more I violate thy laws and keeping the curtains undrawn, sacrifice thee for the last time to that confidence, without reserve, with which I engaged to recount to you the most striking circumstances of my youthful disorders.

As soon, then, as we were in the room together, left to ourselves, the sight of the bed starting the remembrance of our first joys, and the thought of my being instantly to share it with the dear possessor of my virgin heart, mov'd me so strongly, that it was well I lean'd upon him, or I must have fainted again under the overpowering sweet alarm. Charles saw into my confusion, and forgot his own, that was scarce less, to apply himself to the removal of mine.

But now the true refining passion had regain'd thorough possession of me, with all its train of symptoms: a sweet sensibility, a tender timidity, love-sick yearnings temper'd with diffidence and modesty, all held me in a subjection of soul, incomparably dearer to me than the liberty of heart which I had been long, too long! the mistress of, in the course of those grosser gallantries, the consciousness of which now made me sigh with a virtuous confusion and regret. No real virgin, in view of the nuptial bed, could give more bashful blushes to unblemish'd innocence than I did to a sense of guilt; and indeed I lov'd Charles too truly not to feel severely that I did not deserve him.

As I kept hesitating and disconcerted under this soft distraction, Charles, with a fond impatience, took the pains to undress me; and all I can remember amidst the flutter and discomposure of my senses was some flattering exclamations of joy and admiration, more specially at the feel of my breasts, now set at liberty form my stays, and which panting and rising in tumultuous throbs, swell'd upon his dear touch, and gave it the welcome pleasure of finding them well form'd, and unfail'd in firmness.

I was soon laid in bed, and scarce languish'd an instant for the darling partner of it, before he was undress'd and got between the sheets, with his arms clasp'd round me, giving and taking, with gust inexpressible, a kiss of welcome, that my heart rising to my lips stamp'd with its warmest impression, concurring to by bliss, with that delicate and voluptuous emotion which Charles alone had the secret to excite, and which constitutes the very life, the essence of pleasure.

Meanwhile, two candles lighted on a side-table near us, and a joyous wood-fire, threw a light into the bed that took from one sense, of great importance to our joys, all pretext for complaining of its being shut out of its share of them; and indeed, the sight of my idolized youth was alone, from the ardour with which I had wished for it, without other circumstance, a pleasure to die of.

But as action was now a necessity to desires so much on edge as ours, Charles, after a very short prelusive dalliance, lifting up my linen and his own, laid the broad treasures of his manly chest close to my bosom, both beating with the tenderest alarms: when now, the sense of his glowing body, in naked touch with mine, took all power over my thoughts out of my own disposal, and deliver'd up every faculty of the soul to the sensiblest of joys, that affecting me infinitely more with my distinction of the person than of the sex, now brought my conscious heart deliciously into play: my heart, which eternally constant to Charles, had never taken any part in my occasional sacrifices to the calls of constitution, complaisance, or interest. But ah! what became of me, when as the powers of solid pleasure thickened upon me, I could not help feeling the stiff stake that had been adorn'd with the trophies of my despoil'd virginity, bearing hard and inflexible against one of my thighs, which I had not yet opened, from a true principle of modesty, reviv'd by a passion too sincere to suffer any aiming at the false merit of difficulty, or my putting on an impertinent mock coyness.

I have, I believe, somewhere before remark'd, that the feel of that favourite piece of manhood has, in the very nature of it, something inimitably pathetic. Nothing can be dearer to the touch, nor can affect it with a more delicious sensation. Think then! as a love thinks, what must be the consummate transport of that quickest of our senses, in their central seat

Fanny Hill Vol II

too! when, after so long a deprival, it felt itself re-inflam'd under the pressure of that peculiar scepter-member which commands us all: but especially my darling, elect from the face of the whole earth. And now, at its mightiest point of stiffness, it felt to me something so subduing, so active, so solid and agreeable, that I know not what name to give its singular impression: but the sentiment of consciousness of its belonging to my supremely beloved youth, gave me so pleasing an agitation, and work'd so strongly on my soul, that it sent all its sensitive spirits to that organ of bliss in me, dedicated to its reception. There, concentreing to a point, like rays in a burning glass, they glow'd, they burnt with the intensest heat; the springs of pleasure were, in short, wound up to such a pitch, I panted now, with so exquisitely keen an appetite for the eminent enjoyment that I was even sick with desire, and unequal to support the combination of two distinct ideas, that delightfully distracted me: for all the thought I was capable of, was that I was now in touch, at once, with the instrument of pleasure, and the great-seal of love. Ideas that, mingling streams, pour'd such an ocean of intoxicating bliss on a weak vessel, all too narrow to contain it, that I lay overwhelm'd, absorbed, lost in an abyss of joy, and dying of nothing but immoderate delight.

Charles then rous'd me somewhat out of this ecstatic distraction with a complaint softly murmured, amidst a crowd of kisses, at the position, not so favourable to his desires, in which I receiv'd his urgent insistance for admission, where that insistance was alone so engrossing a pleasure that it made me inconsistently suffer a much dearer one to be kept out; but how sweet to correct such a mistake! My thighs, now obedient to the intimations of love and nature, gladly disclose, and with a ready submission, resign up the soft gateway to the entrance of pleasure: I see, I feel the delicious velvet tip! – he enters me might and main, with – oh! my pen drops from me here in the ecstasy now present to my faithful memory! Description too deserts me, and delivers over a task, above its strength of wing, to the imagination: but it must be an imagination exalted by such a flame as mine that can do justice to that sweetest, noblest of all sensations, that hailed and accompany'd the stiff insinuation all the way up, till it was at the end of its penetration, sending up, through my eyes, the sparks of the love-fire that ran all over me and blaz'd in every vein and every pore of me: a system incarnate of joy all over.

I had now totally taken in love's true arrow from the point up to the feather, in that part where, making no new wound, the lips of the original one of nature, which had owed its first breathing to this dear instrument, clung, as if sensible of gratitude, in eager suction round it, whilst all its inwards embrac'd it tenderly with a warmth of gust, a compressive energy, that gave it, in its way, the heartiest welcome in nature; every fibre there gathering tight round it, and straining ambitiously to come in for its share of the blissful touch.

As we were giving them a few moments of pause to the delectation of the senses, in dwelling with the highest relish on this intimatest point of re-union, and chewing the cud of enjoyment, the impatience natural to the pleasure soon drove us into action. Then began the driving tumult on his side, and the responsive heaves on mine, which kept me up to him; whilst, as our joys grew too great for utterance, the organs of our voices, voluptuously intermixing, became organs of the touch – and oh, that touch! how delicious! – how poignantly luscious! – And now! now I felt to the heart of me! I felt the prodigious keen edge with which love, presiding over this act, points the pleasure: love! that may be styled the Attic salt of enjoyment; and indeed, without it, the joy, great as it is, is still a vulgar one, whether in a king or a beggar; for it is, undoubtedly, love alone that refines, ennobles and exalts it.

Thus happy, then, by the heart, happy by the senses, it was beyond all power, even of thought, to form the conception of a greater delight than what I was now consummating the fruition of.

Charles, whose whole frame was convulsed with the agitation of his rapture, whilst the tenderest fires trembled in his eyes, all assured me of a prefect concord of joy, penetrated me so profoundly, touch'd me so vitally, took me so much out of my own possession, whilst he seem'd himself so much in mine, that in a delicious enthusiasm, I imagin'd such a transfusion of heart and spirit, as that coalescing, and making one body and soul with him, I was he, and he, me.

But all this pleasure tending, like life from its first instants, towards its own dissolution, liv'd too fast not to bring on upon the spur its delicious moment of mortality; for presently the approach of the tender agony discover'd itself by its usual signals, that were quickly follow'd by my dear love's emanation of himself that spun out, and shot, feelingly indeed! up the ravish'd in-draught: where the sweetly soothing balmy titillation opened all the juices of joy on my side, which ecstatically in flow, help'd to allay the prurient glow, and drown'd our pleasure for a while. Soon, however, to be on float again! For Charles, true to nature's laws, in one breath expiring and ejaculating, languish'd not long in the dissolving trance, but recovering spirit again, soon gave me to feel that the true-mettle springs of his instrument of pleasure were, by love, and perhaps by a long vacation, wound up too high to be let down by a single explosion: his stiffness still stood my friend. Resuming then the action afresh, without dislodging, or giving me the trouble of parting from my sweet tenant, we play'd over again the same opera, with the same delightful harmony and concert: our ardours, like our love, knew no remission; and, all as the tide serv'd my lover, lavish of his stores, and pleasure milked, overflowed me once more from the fullness of his oval reservoirs of the genial emulsion: whilst, on my side, a convulsive grasp, in the instant of my giving down the liquid contribution, render'd me sweetly subservient at once to the increase of his joy, and of its effusions: moving me so, as to make me exert all those springs of the compressive exsuction with which the sensitive mechanism of that part thirstily draws and drains the nipple of Love; with much such an instinctive eagerness and attachment as, to compare great with less, kind nature engages infants at the breast by the pleasure they find in the motion of their little mouths and cheeks, to extract the milky stream prepar'd for their nourishment.

But still there was no end of his vigour: this double discharge had so far from extinguish'd his desires, for that time, that it had not even calm'd them; and at his age, desires are power. He was proceeding then amazingly to push it to a third triumph, still without uncasing, if a tenderness, natural to true love, had not inspir'd me with self-denial enough to spare, and not overstrain him: and accordingly, entreating him to give himself and me quarter, I obtain'd, at length, a short suspension of arms, but not before he had exultingly satisfy'd me that he gave out standing.

The remainder of the night, with what we borrow'd upon the day, we employ'd with unweary'd fervour in celebrating thus the festival of our re-meeting; and got up pretty late in the morning, gay, brisk and alert, though rest had been a stranger to us: but the pleasures of love had been to us, what the joy of victory is to an army; repose, refreshment, everything.

The journey into the country being now entirely out of the question, and orders having been given over-night for turning the horses' heads towards London, we left the inn as soon as we had breakfasted, not without a liberal distribution of the tokens of my grateful sense of the happiness I had met with in it.

Charles and I were in my coach; the captain and my companion in a chaise hir'd purposely for them, to leave us the conveniency of a *tête-à-tête*.

Here, on the road, as the tumult of my senses was tolerably compos'd, I had command enough to head to break properly to him the course of life that the consequence of my separation from him had driven me into: which, at the same time that he tenderly deplor'd with me, he was the less shocked at; as, on reflecting how he had left me circumstanc'd, he could not be entirely unprepar'd for it.

But when I opened the state of my fortune to him, and with that sincerity which, from me to him, was so much a nature in me, I begg'd of him his acceptance of it, on his own terms. I should appear to you perhaps too partial to my passion, were I to attempt the doing his delicacy justice. I shall content myself then with assuring you, that after his flatly refusing the unreserv'd, unconditional donation that I long persecuted him in vain to accept, it was at length, in obedience to his serious commands (for I stood out unaffectedly, till he exerted the sovereign authority which love had given him over me), that I yielded my consent to waive the remonstrance I did not fail of making strongly to him, against his degrading himself, and incurring the reflection, however unjust, of having, for respects of fortune, barter'd his honour for infamy and prostitution, in making one his wife, who thought herself too much honour'd in being but his mistress.

The plea of love then over-ruling all objections, Charles, entirely won with the merit of my sentiments for him, which he could not but read the sincerity of in a heart ever open to him, oblig'd me to receive his hand, by which means I was in pass, among other innumerable blessings, to bestow a legal parentage on those fine children you have seen by this happiest of matches.

Thus at length, I got snug into port, where, in the bosom of virtue, I gather'd the only uncorrupt sweets: where, looking back on the course of vice I had run, and comparing its infamous blandishments with the infinitely superior joys of innocence, I could not help pitying, even in point of taste, those who, immers'd in gross sensuality, are insensible to the so delicate charms of VIRTUE, than which even PLEASURE has not a greater friend, nor than VICE a greater enemy. Thus temperance makes men lords over those pleasures that intemperance enslaves them to: the one, parent of health, vigour, fertility, cheerfulness, and every other desirable good of life; the other, of diseases, debility, barrenness, self-loathing, with only every evil incident to human nature.

You laugh, perhaps, at this tail-piece of morality, extracted from me by the force of truth, resulting from compar'd experiences: you think it, no doubt, out of place, out of character; possibly too you may look on it as the paltry finesse of one who seeks to mask a devotee to vice under a rag of a veil, impudently smuggled from the shrine of virtue: just as if one was to fancy one's self completely disguised at a masquerade, with no other change of dress than turning one's shoes into slippers; or, as if a writer should think to shield a treasonable libel, by concluding it with a formal prayer for the King. But, independent of my flattering myself that you have a juster opinion of my sense and sincerity, give me leave to represent to you, that such a supposition is even more injurious to virtue than to me: since, consistently with candour and good-nature, it can have no foundation but in the falsest of fears, that its pleasures cannot stand in comparison with those of vice; but let truth dare to hold it up in its most alluring light: then mark, how spurious, how low of taste, how comparatively inferior its joys are to those which virtue gives sanction to, and whose sentiments are not above making even a sauce for the senses, but a sauce of the highest relish; whilst vices are the harpies that infect and foul the feast. The paths of vice are sometimes strew'd with roses, but then they are for ever infamous for many a thorn, for many a canker-worm: those of virtue are strew'd with roses purely, and those eternally unfading ones.

If you do me then justice, you will esteem me perfectly consistent in the incense I burn to virtue. If I have painted vice in all its gayest colours, if I have deck'd it with flowers, it has been solely in order to make the worthier, the solemner sacrifice of it, to virtue.

You know Mr. C—— O——, you know his estate, his worth, and good sense: can you, will you pronounce it ill meant, at least of him, when anxious for his son's morals, with a view to form him to virtue, and inspire him with a fix'd, a rational contempt for vice, he condescended to be his master of the ceremonies, and led him by the hand thro' the most noted bawdy-houses in town, where he took care he should be familiarised with all those scenes of debauchery, so fit to nauseate a good taste? The experiment, you will cry, is dangerous. True, on a fool: but are fools worth so much attention?

I shall see you soon, and in the mean time think candidly of me, and believe me ever,

MADAM,

Yours, &c., &c., &c.

FIN

The Scarlet Library

At the Erotic Print Society, we think that books can and should be decently made. That is why we created the Scarlet Library: the most sensuous and shamelessly erotic books available today.

Beatrice
GORDON GRIMLEY
with new illustrations by
LYNN PAULA RUSSELL

Eveline
ANONYMOUS
with new illustrations by
VANIA ZOURAVLIOV

Gamiani
ALFRED DE MUSSET
with new illustrations by
VANIA ZOURAVLIOV

Letters from a Friend in Paris
ANONYMOUS
with new illustrations by
MICHAEL FARADAY

A Night in a Moorish Harem
ANONYMOUS
with illustrations by
HARRY DOUGLAS

Séduction
ANONYMOUS
with new illustrations by
SYLVIE JONES

The Simple Tale of Susan Aked
ANONYMOUS
with new illustrations by
CHRIS PRICE

Summer in the Country
AUGUSTE POULET-MALASSIS
with new illustrations by
ADRIAN GEORGE

Two Flappers in Paris
ANONYMOUS
with new illustrations by
SOPHIE ALEXANDER

A Weekend Visit
ANONYMOUS
with new illustrations by
TIM MAJOR

The Way of a Man with a Maid
ANONYMOUS
with new illustrations by
TIM MAJOR

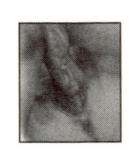

The Autobiography of a Flea
ANONYMOUS
with new illustrations by
MARK RICHFIELD

THE SCARLET LIBRARY books are available through the Erotic Print Society. Please call us for a free catalogue on 0871 7110 134, or visit our website at www.eroticprints.org